Tomorrow's Promise

Bernadette Piper

i

A catalogue record for this book is available from the National Library of Australia

Linellen Press
265 Boomerang Road
Oldbury, Western Australia
www.linellenpress.com.au

Dedication

For my children and their children

Contents

Acknowledgments

Thank you once more to Helen Iles for your help and suggestion in bringing this story to life.

Prologue

Fremantle.
Western Australia.
April 1969

Cold salty air slapped his face as he tugged his coat together, squashed his hat securely down on his grey hair and strode down the pathway towards his home.

The girl sat on the bench beneath the Eucalyptus tree, her limp blonde hair blowing around her face. He stopped. She looked up at him, her eyes red, her face stained with tears. He held out his hand and said, 'Come in out of the rain.'

She dragged her rucksack off the ground, pulled it over her shoulder and took his hand.

Rain began to fall. He tried to hurry but the girl didn't seem to care, her cheesecloth blouse and long floral skirt already wet. She wasn't dressed for the cold weather that had come in over the ocean.

He put his key in the lock. The girl glanced around, then ran her hands through her hair. The world had gone grey since he'd left home that morning, the last of the summer warmth had gone, the smell of wet grass washed away by continual rain. Flowers and plants drooped, and the birds were quiet.

Warm air surrounded them when he opened the front door of his home. He guided her into his kitchen, sat her on a chair, took the blanket he kept by the stove for cold nights and wrapped it around her shoulders. He stirred the logs till the flames caught, then moved the kettle to the middle of the stove. The girl sat silent, her eyes watching him, her body motionless.

He placed the teapot and cups on the table in front of her and sat on the chair opposite. She took the cup he'd poured and wrapped her shaking hands around it while he waited for her to talk, but she stayed silent staring into the flames. He could wait, did not want to pry, wanted her to feel safe, to trust him, to warm up. He waited, then finally she said, 'I'll go to hell.'

'Why? What have you done that is so bad?' he asked.

The girl looked across the table at him; she pushed her tears away with her fingertips. 'Would God forgive me if I killed my unborn child?' she asked.

'Tell me.'

She looked back at the fire, her fingers in her mouth. 'I was stupid, I trusted him. I loved him … he said he loved me, and I believed him. He said he would come back for me. What else can I do?'

'You don't have to do that … there are other options,' he said to comfort her. The girl turned to face him, pushed her wet hair behind her ears.

'Does he know?' he asked.

'I tried to tell him; he didn't answer my letters. He didn't even open them.'

She rummaged around in her rucksack, pulled out a crumpled envelope, put it on the table in front of her.

'I trusted him. He didn't open my letters; he lied to me.' She shook her head, pulled herself upright, let the blanket fall and pushed herself from the chair. 'I have to go.'

'Stay for a while … we can talk.'

'No, I have to go.'

Picking up her rucksack, she hurried down the passage and out the front door.

He followed her, but by the time he reached the front door,

he could not see her in the darkening autumn dusk – even on a bright sunny day, his eyes let him down.

There being nothing he could do, he returned to the kitchen. The girl had not picked up the envelope, and he read the name on the front.

'He did not lie to you,' Father Francis Kelly said.

Chapter One

December 1968
Perth, Western Australia

Emmaline

Emmy's ears hurt as drums banged, tambourines clashed and chinked, and voices chanted as the small group of no more than twenty she was a part of carried placards and sang peace songs as they marched in the dust and dirt along St Georges Terrace. Office workers and shoppers crossed the street to avoid the group. Someone called them '*A mob of long hair layabouts,*' but they weren't. They were all working or studying.

The group stopped in front of a building housing the United States of America Consulate, a red brick building with six steps leading to a portico and a double jarrah door.

Emmy's hair blew into her eyes, and her long floral skirt wrapped around her knees; her calico blouse did nothing to stop the cold. Emmy had never attended a demonstration before. She didn't know much about war as her parents kept their past hidden from Emmy and her brothers.

What Emmy did know was her brother would be turning twenty next year. If his birthdate was drawn out of a lottery, he would have to join the army and go to Vietnam. He could die in Vietnam; Mama would not survive if that happened. Emmy had to protect her family; she had to do what she could to keep her brother safe, like she'd done since she was twelve years old. She wasn't here protesting those who fought and died; she wanted the war to end; she didn't want her brother to die in Vietnam. Emmy wanted the soldiers to come home.

Hoping for a time when children could grow without the threat of war, her placard read: NO MORE WAR, but she knew while old men sent young men to die, nothing would change. Barry McGuire's *Eve of Destruction, you're old enough to kill but not for voting* echoed around her mind.

A wreath of flowers, a symbol of lives lost, was to be placed at the consulate door. Some of the boys had wanted to bring pig blood to throw, but Emmy had refused to be part of that.

Several policemen stood on the portico, tapping batons on the palms of their hands.

Emmy joined the demonstrators carrying the wreath up the stairs. They were naïve. The police moved down the steps towards them; the tapping of the batons became a heavy thud. The police charged into the group of demonstrators, bringing their batons down hard. Emmy saw her friends knocked to the ground, dragged away, their faces covered in blood. Her placard destroyed, she saw the wreath trampled to pieces and grabbed a handful of broken flowers. Making her way to the portico, she tripped and fell.

Emmy could hear the thud, thud, thud of a baton on a palm. She looked into the face of the person holding the baton and saw hate. She covered her head with her arms.

A shadow fell over her and she glimpsed a white uniform; tumbled into brown eyes. A voice said, 'Go.'

Emmy struggled to her feet and ran. She heard the same voice say, 'I don't think you want to do that.'

She did not look back.

Sitting with her legs dangling over the cement wall on the river embankment, she still shook but had stopped gulping for air. Her heart no longer felt like it was trying to get out of her chest – she hadn't run so fast or so far since she'd been in high school. Her sprint along St Georges Terrace, across the grass of the Esplanade and down Barrack Street to the river had startled lunchtime workers.

'Emmy.'

She jumped.

'Emmy, are you alright?'

'I'm okay, Jacob. Are you?'

'Yes,' he said as he sat on the wall beside her.

'You don't look it.' Emmy reached out and pushed Jacob's blond hair back. Blood stuck to her fingers. He ran his hand through his hair, his blue eyes still showing shock from the blow. His checked shirt was torn, and blood splattered his flared jeans.

'What happened? We were peaceful. We have a right to demonstrate. How could the police hate us so much?' Emmy asked.

Jacob shrugged and put his arm around her.

'What about the others?' Emmy asked.

'Charlie got arrested.'

'His dad's not going to be happy.'

'Nah,' he said.

Emmy rested against Jacob and stared across the river, watching a ferry making its way to the jetty on the other side of the river. Normal everyday occurrences on a day that hadn't turned out as she'd expected. Small windblown waves threatened their feet, and Emmy pushed herself off the ground. Jacob helped her up.

'Damn,' Emmy said and tipped her bag upside down.

'What's wrong?'

Keys and a compact lay on the ground, bits of sweet wrapper blew away. 'I've lost my purse,' she said.

'Did you have much in it?'

'Only bus fare. Oh hell, my learner's permit, with my name and address on it.'

Chapter Two

Emmaline

There was a knock on the door. Little feet padded down the wooden hallway and opened it.

'Emmy, your boyfriend's here,' a little boy called.

'I don't have a boyfriend, Joey,' Emmy said as she came to the door.

She tickled him under his arms, and he pulled away and skipped down the hallway, chanting, 'Emmy's got a boyfriend. Emmy's got a boyfriend.'

Emmy stared into the eyes of the man standing at the front door. 'Oh!' she said.

'Who is it, Emmy?' her mother called from the kitchen. 'Is it one of your friends from yesterday?'

The man in front of her wore a blue and white checked shirt tucked into a pair of pressed Levi jeans. His dark curls were cut short, and his black shoes were clean and polished.

'Sort of, Mama,' she said and pulled the front door closed behind her as she joined him on the veranda.

Emmy remembered his eyes. Eyes that in the moment they locked with hers saw too much of her. If she hadn't been afraid and trying to protect herself, she would have wondered what was happening.

'Am I in trouble?' she asked.

Now she wondered what was happening.

'Well,' he said. 'Are you Emmaline Marie Cannon?'

'Yes.'

He held her purse in his hands, reading her details from her learner's permit.

'So?' she said.

'Let's see. Will you come for coffee with me?'

Coffee! What was he talking about? She could be in big trouble here – he spoke with an American accent and was in a uniform yesterday!

He'd stopped the baton from hitting her.

Micky

Michael Francis Brannigan stood on the front veranda of a little weatherboard cottage on Fairlight Street in Mosman Park.

The girl in front of him wore a long floral skirt and a white blouse, her blonde hair falling down her back. She had small flowers braided through the plaits at the front, and a headband of flowers sat on her forehead. Her hazel eyes stared into his, confused and bewildered by his question. He couldn't believe he'd said that. She must think he was an idiot or so full of himself.

He said: 'I'm sorry. I didn't mean to say that. I only wanted to return your purse. My name is Michael Brannigan.' He held out his hand, and she shook it. He added, 'I picked it up yesterday. No one else has seen it. I don't think you will be in trouble.'

The warm summer breeze blew strands of her hair across her face; he wanted to push it back, away from her eyes. But he'd already made a fool of himself, he should have just given her purse back. What was he thinking?

She pushed the hair away from her eyes and said, 'Yes.'

'Yes?'

She still held his hand, still stared into his eyes.

'I would like to have coffee with you.' Then she said, 'I have to get some shoes on though.' She let go of his hand, opened the front door and went back into the house.

He sat on the top of the two steps that lead to the veranda, the shade of the eucalyptus tree that stood on the green lawn to one side of a cement pathway keeping him cool.

The front door opened, and he started to stand to greet her. The little boy with his mop of blond hair sat on the step beside him. 'Are you Emmy's boyfriend?' he asked.

'No,' he said. 'We have just met.'

'What's your name?' the boy asked.

'Michael, but my friends call me Micky.'

'Like Mickey Mouse?'

He laughed. 'Yes, I guess so,' he said.

Emmaline came out the front door and said, 'Jimmy, don't be a pest.'

'Twins?' he queried.

'Twins,' she said.

'It's okay,' he said. 'I was a little brother – my sisters spoilt me rotten.' Those memories always made him smile.

'Same here, I'm afraid.'

'Micky's Emmy's boyfriend. Micky's Emmy's boyfriend.' The little boy chanted again as he stood from the step.

'Jimmy!' Emmy scolded. 'Don't be cheeky.' Her cheeks flushed with pink, which she tried to hide.

'Sorry about that,' she said and ran her hands through her hair.

'It's okay.' He could feel the warmth in his face.

'Go inside, Jimmy,' Emmaline said. 'You are not allowed out here on your own. You know Mama will worry.'

Chapter Three

Emmaline

Emmaline and Michael sat at a table covered in a red and white checked cloth in the window of Luige's coffee shop on South Street in Fremantle.

How odd they must look. Michael's hair short, his clothing neat and conservative, his black shoes clean and polished. Emmaline with flowers in her braids and beads around her neck, old Dunlop tennis shoes on her feet.

'Thank you,' Emmy said.

'For what?'

'Not dobbing me in.'

'I couldn't let that happen,' he said.

'Are you American?' Emmy asked. 'Your accent's a bit strange.'

'Yes. My mother is Australian. I picked up some Aussie accent from her and my sister. We got teased about our accent a bit at school when we were little.'

Emmy turned to the waiter and said, 'Ciao, Tony, can we have some of your wonderful coffee.'

Then she said to Michael, 'This is the best place for coffee in Fremantle. Most people here still drink tea but Mama and Papa like coffee, so we have always come here. Do you drink tea or coffee?' *What on earth was she saying?*

He answered her question with a smile, then said, 'We drink coffee and tea at home in the US. My mother likes to drink tea, I think it reminds her of her home in Fremantle. We drink a lot of tea when we visit family in Australia. We were here last year.'

A sadness crossed his face. 'Grandparents die,' he said.

'I suppose so,' Emmy said.

He shook his head and said, 'So, Emmaline Marie Cannon, what do you do when you are not throwing flowers at the American Consulate?'

'I'm a teacher,' Emmy said. 'I graduated Teachers College this year. I have a posting in a country town called Wagin starting next year.'

Michael said, 'It's important to you.'

'Oh yes, it's important to me,' Emmy said. Sister Joan used the ruler as a weapon, and Emmy was terrified of her, of going to school, afraid for her brother. Children shouldn't have to learn like that, and Emmy knew she could make a difference, make learning easier, and safer for children. 'I've wanted to be a teacher since I was a little girl, my dream come true. It wasn't easy though. I had to work hard. It took me a long time to catch up after …'

Why was she telling Michael this; her secrets were not shared with anyone. Why was it so easy to tell Micky?

Emmy pulled herself together and said, 'I'm glad you didn't dob me in. I could get into a lot of trouble.'

'I wouldn't do that.' He smiled across the table at her.

Emmy wanted to ask him why but said, 'What do you do?'

'I'm a Corpsman.'

'What's that?' Emmy asked.

'A Medic in the Navy.'

'The American Navy?'

'Yes.'

This could be a mistake. She'd spent yesterday at a protest against the Vietnam War, against conscription and the United States military.

Her eyes met his across the table. Those eyes had looked into hers yesterday, seen into her yesterday. Micky had taken a great risk for her, and he didn't know her.

She asked him, 'Have you been to Vietnam?'

'No, not yet.'

'Emmy!' Jacob came in the front door of the café.

'Emmy, look! You're in the paper.' He held a copy of the *West Australian*. The headline read. WHO IS THE ENEMY?

The picture showed a policeman, his face blotted out, his baton held ready to strike a cowering girl, a girl covering her head with her arm. Stopping the blow from falling on the girl was an American sailor who had his back to the camera.

Jacob noticed Michael.

'What are you doing here with him? I saw him yesterday at the protest, in a uniform,' he said. He grabbed her arm. 'Come home now.'

'No, Jacob,' she said.

'He's a baby killer. How can you sit here with him?'

Yes, they'd all seen the pictures in the paper and the stories on the news. If their protest yesterday could make any difference, make one politician think, make one policeman lower his baton, save one life, it would be worth it. That Micky was the sailor in the picture, his back to the camera, Jacob did not know.

'Jacob!' Emmy cried and pulled her arm away.

Micky leapt to his feet, grabbed Jacob by the arm and said, 'The lady said no.'

Jacob swung his fist.

Tony stopped the blow. 'Come on, Jacob, you should leave.' He escorted Jacob to the door and pulled him out onto the street. Words, unheard from inside, were spoken and Jacob left.

'I'm sorry,' Emmy said. 'I should leave.'

It was a mistake: he was an American sailor; she shouldn't have come out with him. Emmy rose from her chair and Micky caught her hand.

'Please don't,' he said.

And there it was again, her hand in his. Lightning raced up her arm, her heart jumped, and her body trembled. She needed to take control. She brushed her cheek with the back of her other hand. She knew nothing about Micky, she'd only just met him, yet she sat back in her chair.

'Are you okay?' he asked. His eyes full of concern, he reached across the table and touched where the tears had sat on her cheeks; she wished he hadn't; his fingers on her cheeks confused her.

Emmy nodded.

'Okay, Bella?' Tony asked. He stopped and put his arms around her shoulders.

'Okay, Tony,' Emmy said.

She held Tony's arms tight across her shoulders. Her friend, safe and unthreatening, she'd worked with him at the café when she was younger.

The café returned to its usual Saturday afternoon trade, people at other tables whispering behind their hands.

'I'm sorry,' Emmy repeated.

'He cares about you,' Micky said.

'I care about him … Jacob's had a much harder life than most of us. His parents died in the war. His grandmother bought him up. Papa's been like a father to him; he got him an apprenticeship at the car factory. He's like a brother to me, and I care about him, but I don't want to be his girlfriend. I don't love him like that.'

'How can you be sure?' he asked

'If you have to ask, that's your answer,' Emmy said.

A smile ran across Micky's face. His straight chin and dimples made him look like a cheeky little boy who could get away with most things, like her twin brothers.

'What?' Emmy asked.

'They are the exact words my father used when I asked him

the same question,' Micky said.

Emmy smiled at that. Yes you shouldn't have to ask that question; but could it be that simple?

'He thinks you do?' Micky asked.

'Maybe, I don't know.'

Tony bought more coffee.

'We've grown up together; his grandmother and Mama are friends. They both speak German. Jacob has started acting strange since we … I got older,' Emmy said.

Micky smiled at that.

'Were you conscripted?' Emmy asked.

'No, my father was in the Navy, so I joined up. I didn't want to go to the Academy and be an officer. I don't want to carry a weapon, so being a corps … a medic suits me. My Australian grandfather was a medic at Gallipoli. I am proud of who I am and what I do. I know what I do is important.'

'Yes. We never think of that, do we,' Emmy said.

'You wouldn't know.'

'Maybe we should. I'm sorry he said those awful things about you,' she said.

'It's okay. Medics save lives, not take them,' Micky said.

Emmy stared into his eyes. If she let him, he would see into her soul; if she didn't, she could walk away. She turned her head and looked out the window.

Micky

Michael Brannigan regarded the girl sitting opposite him. He'd been coming out of the consulate when he'd seen the baton held high; he couldn't let that blow fall, so he had intervened. When her frightened and confused eyes had looked up at him, he'd been surprised, caught off guard.

She'd raced away down the Terrace, and he had to deal with an angry Australian policeman. He couldn't follow her but needed to find out who she was, so he'd put his foot on her purse to hide it. He'd never done anything like that before, never been so *smitten,* such an old fashion word but what else could he use.

After coffee, Emmaline had shopping to do. Across the road was an old red and brick building, the FREMANTLE MARKETS, it said on the wall. She bought groceries and they shared an ice cream. He carried her bags as they strolled past the town hall with its clock on the tower, down the High Street to the railway station. He had offered to take Emmaline home in a taxi, but she insisted on taking the train.

On the platform, he couldn't let her go; he wanted to see her again and said, 'Will you come to dinner with me tonight?'

'I can't,' she said.

His heart skipped. Had he misunderstood? She came from a different world to him, but she'd stayed in the café with him, her ideals in conflict.

His surprise when she'd looked into his eyes, the way his heart pounded when Emmaline had shaken his hand, had astounded him; nothing like this had ever happened to him before. He couldn't let her walk out of his life.

'I have a party to go to,' she said. 'Would you like to come?'

Her friends would have similar views to those Jacob expressed. Nevertheless, he said, 'Yes.'

Chapter Four

Micky

At the bottom of a driveway overlooking the ocean on West Coast Highway, Micky stood holding Emmaline's hand.

He had rummaged around in his kit bag and found a floral Hawaiian shirt to wear and had scrunched up his jeans. There was nothing he could do about his hair, so he'd given up on it.

Emmaline had dressed in burnt orange, waist-high flares and a sequined white halter neck top. On her feet, she wore wedged shoes. She had removed the braids and headband from her hair but wore some flowers twisted through the loose strands. Still a flower girl, not so much a hippie.

Emmaline told him the party was to celebrate the end of three years at Teachers College. They would all be going to different country towns next year; most of them would be working Christmas jobs until then.

The party was in full swing: music blared out of the undercroft parking area, people milled around drinking and talking.

Emmaline introduced him to her friend, a stunning dark-haired girl named Julie. 'Well, aren't you the cutest thing ever?' Julie said. 'Where did you find him, Emmy?'

The Beach Boys were playing *Surfing USA* on the record player. Julie pulled his hand from Emmy's and dragged him into the middle of the garage that was being used as a dance floor. She put her arms around his neck and ground her hips into his. While he didn't want to be rude, he didn't want to dance with her either. Over her shoulder, he saw Emmy leave.

Emmaline

Emmy meandered along the coast road alone under the dull streetlights. She could hear Normie Rowe's *Shaking All Over* playing on the record player. Breakers on the shore rumbled in. There weren't many cars on the road but sometimes one would slow down, and someone would whistle. Emmy hated that. She knew for most of the boys it was harmless, meant as a compliment, but it always made her feel vulnerable and unsafe.

'Emmaline, please. Please wait for me.'

She stopped beneath a streetlight and turned to face him. Why had it bothered her so much? She shouldn't be so upset. Julie always got all the attention.

Pretty and petite, with dark hair curling down her back, Julie had become a woman at sixteen while Emmy, at five foot eight, was still an awkward, gangly girl with mousy blonde hair. Emmy was used to it; she never expected anyone to notice her when Julie was around. She really didn't mind – she had other things she needed to do – but she thought Michael was different.

'Julie always does that; it doesn't normally bother me,' she said.

Micky took her face in his hands and put his lips to hers, his tongue exploring, seeking. Emmy put her arms around his neck and opened her lips. She'd never kissed like that before, never wanted to kiss like that before, she'd never let anyone hold her so tight. His body wove its way around her. Emmy leaned into his body, holding herself upright.

A passing car slowed, and a voice called, 'Get a room.'

They pulled apart, laughing.

'Let's get out of here,' Micky said.

The Windsor Night Club was downstairs in a basement on Hay Street, the doorman asked Emmy's age, but Micky was full of bluster.

'Come on, man, half my shipmates are here tonight. I'll take care of the young lady,' he said.

Micky was right: the nightclub was full of sailors, some in uniform, some not. From the top of the staircase, Emmy could see through the smoke-filled air tables and chairs full of people. A bar to one side of the room had people leaning against it, the odour of alcohol saturated the air. The Troupers, so it said on the drum kit, were playing soul music, songs by Otis Redding and Sam Cooke.

Micky put his arm around Emmy as they went down the stairs heading for a table away from the dance floor. He introduced her to his shipmates. William shook her hand; Simon brushed his lips on the back of her hand before holding a chair out for her. Emmy refused alcohol – she wasn't old enough – so the boys ordered her Coca-Cola without making a fuss.

Emmy danced all night. She had a dance with Simon, but most of the time she danced with William for when the band started playing and Emmy swayed in her chair, William immediately stood and offered his hand. That confused Emmy; she didn't need Micky's permission to dance with William, but he was the one she'd come to the nightclub with.

William leant forward and whispered in her ear, 'These white boys can't dance.'

Micky's grin told Emmy he knew exactly what William had said. Micky and Simon continued talking.

The girls of Perth were having fun with the sailors from Micky's ship. She saw two of them sashay over to Simon and Micky, enticing them to dance. Simon held up his left hand to show his wedding ring; Micky smiled and shook his head. When the band played Otis Redding's *These Arms of Mine,* Micky took Emmy in his arms and wrapped his body around her. They left the club rather late.

Emmy tiptoed up the steps onto the front veranda. The porch light was still on, and she realised she must be the first one home. Micky insisted on walking her to the front door, and she turned to his friends sitting in the waiting taxi and put her finger to her lips.

'Can I see you tomorrow?' Micky whispered.

'Emmy, is that you?' her father called.

'Yes, Papa.'

'Is Hank with you?'

'No, Papa.'

'Papa always knows when we get home,' she whispered. 'I'm taking the twins to Cottesloe Beach tomorrow.'

'Can I meet you there?' he said.

'Jacob might be there.'

'That's okay.' He pulled her close and chewed her bottom lip.

'Emmy, what are you doing?' her father called.

'Nothing, Papa. Coming.'

Emmy watched Micky walk down the pathway into the waiting taxi. She touched her lips on the spot he'd been chewing. She'd never done that before.

Emmy had done a lot of things tonight she'd never done before. She opened the unlocked front door and went inside, leaving the light on for her brother.

Chapter Five

Emmaline

Emmy sat on white sands, her skin sizzling in the sun. She had covered herself in coconut oil to promote a tan and the lemon juice she'd used to lighten her hair wafted a gentle fragrance around her. Her portable transistor radio played Billy Thorpe and the Aztec's *Poison Ivy* while her twin brothers tumbled around in the waves. The groyne to the south offered some protection from the swell on the beach, and a little paddle pool for children sat at the end of the overhead shade ramp, but the boys had wanted to swim in the ocean. Every now and then, a large wave would roll in and their little bodies would crash onto the shore. Jimmy had always been more adventurous and ran about laughing while Joey sat crying in the surf. Emmy wrapped Joey in her towel, sat him on her knee and wiped his tears. *One for you and one for Mama*, Papa had said, but it hadn't been.

Emmy kept looking around. Micky said he would meet her this morning; it was getting late and the sea breeze would soon be blowing and they would have to leave. Her mind flicked back … what a night she'd had. ?And how she had loved dancing.

'That's not how to dance,' Papa said and had tried to show her steps he knew.

But it was dancing to Emmy. She enjoyed the music, soul music, Motown music; music she couldn't buy in Perth. She'd had to send to Sydney for an Otis Redding album.

Emmy had never met anyone like the boys she'd spent last night with. She called them *boys*, but they weren't boys; they were men. And that was the difference. She'd only ever gone out with boys. Boys who were always trying to put their hands where she didn't want them; boys who acted like she should be grateful for their attention. She'd spent last night with men.

Simon was the most handsome man she'd ever seen. Tall, slim and fair, with blond hair, piercing blue eyes and a warm, sexy smile. William was taller, with Sidney Poitier dark skin, dark eyes and short dark hair. She'd loved Sidney Poitier in *To Sir With Love*.

And Micky, so beautiful, not as tall as William but taller than Simon, with curly brown hair, cut short, and brown eyes she could fall into and never leave. His smile, so cheeky and gentle, that her heart flipped over when he used it on her, making her forget everything the Sisters at her high school had taught her.

Emmy had spent five years at that high school on the hill in Perth, a school for girls. The first two years were interrupted, but she'd studied hard and had caught up by the time she'd finished third-year high, enough to allow her to continue on and get her Leaving Certificate and go to Teachers College.

She was older now and didn't attend church anymore, except to take the twins to Midnight Mass at Christmas. The lectures still sat in her ears though – no real advice … how could Nuns know. The only thing you learned at school was, Don't.

She let her thoughts turn to Micky, how she had been in his arms, his lips on hers, his body against hers, her body knowing what it wanted, those words in her ears … she was unsure if she could do that.

Two hands covered her eyes from behind, and his voice said, 'What's the matter, little man?'

'My knee.'

Micky sat on the sand beside them and studied the little boy's knee with great concern. 'I'm a Medic, you know. A Medic fixes up injured people. I think your knee will be okay.'

Joey climbed off Emmy's knee and rubbed his injury before

running back into the water to join his brother.

Micky put his arms around Emmy and pulled her close. He kissed her on the lips. How she wanted to stay in his embrace, but she couldn't do that on a hot summer's day, on a crowded beach. His kiss was soft and gentle and appropriate for where they were.

He released his hold on her and, pulling his t-shirt over his head, said, 'Coming in?'

Emmy sucked in her breath at the pale skin tanned by the sun, at the brown curls smattering his chest, and the firm, athletic build, with some of the boyishness yet to grow out. *Amazing, terrifying.* 'Yes,' she said.

She rose from the sand and ran into the water, her hot face cooled by the ocean.

Micky

Micky watched Emmy run into the water. His life was already set out for him; it did not include a girl from the other side of the world. He was a sailor; he was going to war. No girl could be part of that life – he'd made that promise to himself and his mother. Was he keeping it?

Emmy called from the water, 'It's cold.'

He ran into the ocean, diving through an incoming wave and coming up within arm's reach of her and wrapping her into his arms. Emmy's height emphasised her slight build. The top of her head sat just at his shoulder. She wore a two-piece bikini, the oil she had used to promote a tan still warm on her skin; her warm body now locked in his arms. Then he dived away, swimming deeper, out towards the end of the breakwater. He could hear her giggling and calling to the twins as he swam away.

Emmy was standing at the water's edge when he swam back to her; she had a beach towel wrapped around her, protecting her from the sand now being tossed around by the brisk wind blowing.

'Time to go, boys,' she called to the twins. The boys grizzled. 'What are the rules?' she said, shaking her head.

'If we don't come home now, we don't come again,' they said in unison.

'Yes,' she said.

'They are good little boys,' he said. 'Your parents have taught them well.'

'My parents, yes …'

'What?' he asked her

'Nothing.' She shook her head.

'Can I walk home with you?'

'Jacob's going to pick us up in Papa's car. He comes down ten minutes after the wind starts blowing. Please come home with us?'

He shook his head. 'Can I see you later today?'

'I would like that.' She took his hand and he pulled her close. Two little boys ran out of the water, picked up towels and headed up the beach towards the grassed embankment.

'Come on, Emmy,' they called. She pulled out of his arms.

He wasn't keeping his promise to his mother or himself.

Chapter Six

Emmaline

On Monday, December 9th, the sun set into the ocean and turned the sky pink. Emmy and Micky sat on the sand, eating out of paper, Simon and William also sharing a meal between them. Overhead, seagulls hovered and stalked them.

'We are heading out Wednesday morning,' William told her. 'But this lucky jerk gets to stay for another two weeks.' He thumbed towards Micky. 'These boys have friends in high places.'

Micky threw a chip at him, and the seagulls swooped. William waved his arms and shouted at the squawking birds until they took flight.

But Emmy already knew Micky wasn't staying. He was a sailor and would be leaving, and the best thing to do was not think about it.

The meal gone, the boys ran into the darkening water, leaving Emmy sitting alone watching them. *Best not think about it*, but that was hard. She'd never known anyone like Micky. And she already knew the answer to that question, *you do not have to ask*. Her life plan was to go to Wagin after Christmas, to live in a house supplied by the Education Department, to teach children. Her dream come true, a dream that had been hard to reach. She watched the three boys bodysurfing, knowing it would be dark soon. She stood, kicking sand through her toes as she made her way to the water's edge.

'Time to go, boys,' Emmy called.

They grizzled.

'Shark feeding time,' Emmy joked.

It did the trick — they came sprinting out of the ocean, splashing her with water, Emmy standing surrounded by semi-naked male flesh. This wouldn't do, her warm cheeks kept giving her away. Simon and William picked up their towels and jogged up the sand to the grass embankment while Emmy and Micky plopped back onto the sand, Micky wrapping the towel around them both. She curled into his body in the near dark; sought his mouth with open lips. Micky ran his hand around her neck, down the front of her blouse, inside her blouse … she wasn't going to stop him.

In mere seconds, he pulled his hand away and scrambled to his feet. Wrapping the towel around his waist, he said, 'We should go.' His voice sounded different to her.

Emmy didn't understand her feeling of disappointment.

Micky

In 1968, when Micky was twenty-three, there had been girls and women in his life, and there had been relationships, not many, but they had been with women who knew what they were doing. He didn't think the girls in this country could be that different to the women he'd known — he couldn't be sure, but he didn't think so.

But Emmy was different. He should have been more careful, but he had a feeling it was getting too late for that … the promises he'd made to himself, but especially the one he'd made to his mother.

She'd said, 'Don't fall in love before you go to war, Micky. Don't leave a girl behind waiting, alone.'

His mother never spoke of her time during the previous war. He knew his parents had met in Fremantle when his father's submarine was stationed there. He knew his father had suffered serious injuries.

His sisters remembered bits and pieces about that time. There were photographs at home in a special place on the mantle over the fire: his sister Karen's mother and brother – his brother, who had died in a motor accident in 1941. His sister Jessie's father, who'd been killed in the war in 1941. The family kept the pictures and the memory safe but they didn't talk about that time.

Emmy sat before him, confused.

What his mother hadn't told him was how to do that – how to not fall in love.

He took Emmy's hand, helped her up and pulled her close. He should have been more careful; his father was right –you shouldn't have to ask *that question*. They had two more weeks together; he would work it out later.

On Wednesday, he dressed in his white uniform and joined his shipmates aboard the transport ship USNS *Jackson*. She was sailing at 13.00 hours. William was right; he did have friends in high places … or his father did. He'd been able to arrange extra leave for him to visit his grandfather and other family members. He would also visit his mother's friend, a man he'd called Uncle Frank when he was a child. He had been given permission to join the *Jackson* in Singapore, where she was due to leave on December 26th.

Micky stood on the windswept dock and saluted his friends. The ship lifted her anchor, and the tugs began pulling her out of the harbour.

He'd known Simon all his life. They were *navy brats* growing up together, going to school together, getting into mischievous together. Their fathers had served together. Simon's father stilled served in *high places*. William had come into their friendship circle when they were at college, and it always amazed him how well he fitted in, like he'd always been there.

When Simon said goodbye to Becky before they left Pearl Harbour, he was glad he was still single; glad he hadn't met anyone; he was thankful he wasn't going to leave a girl behind. Now what was he going to do?

He met Emmy at the Fremantle railway station and took her to meet his grandfather, his mother's father. He lived on his own now, Grandmother having died last year. They sat on the back veranda and looked out across the garden. His grandfather bought tea on a tray out the backdoor, Micky standing and holding the door open.

'I can manage,' Sean O'Brien said.

'I know, Grandpa.'

Sean sat on the empty chair and poured the tea. 'So, Emmaline, what is it you do?' he asked.

'I'm working at Aherns for Christmas, and then I'm going to Wagin in January. I finished Teacher College this year,' Emmy said proudly.

'And you, my boy, how long are you here for?'

'Not long, Grandpa. I have to leave before Christmas.'

He glanced at Emmy; she was looking at the tea in her cup.

'I miss …'

'I know, Grandpa,' he said. *More than sixty years together.* He had known Emmy for six days. He took his grandfather's hand.

'Your Mother is coming to visit me next year?'

'Yes, in March.'

'When are you going to Vietnam?' his grandfather asked.

'Not sure. Soon, I think,' he replied.

Emmy still looked across the garden to the back fence.

'Be careful.'

'I'm a medic, Grandpa, like you. I'll be okay.'

'Yes, yes. Come, come and look at the garden?'

Emmaline

Emmy sat pushing her feet into the patch of sand in the otherwise green lawn. The swing seat was old but the ropes holding it to the tree were new. Micky strolled around the garden with his grandfather. An old washhouse stood in the backyard, and they stopped to look at the pot plants on a bench beside the building. Micky had his head down in concentration paying attention to his grandfather's words.

Emmy didn't have any grandparents, not ones she could spend time with, share secrets with, share love with. Christmas wasn't far away; she mustn't keep Micky away from his family. Christmas was when Micky would be leaving. She mustn't think about that.

That evening Micky met Emmy's parents.

Mama said, 'What should I cook? What should I say?'

Emmy told her, 'Don't make a fuss, Mama. Micky is a friend, like Jacob. Fill an extra plate for him.'

'He is a guest,' Mama had insisted and prepared her best.

Micky bought flowers for Mama; he helped her carry the dishes to the table and held her chair out for her. He was so handsome in his uniform. Mama liked Micky. Papa shook the hand Micky offered him and gave him the look only a father could, so many questions without a word spoken. The twins ran around the house like they always did, and Hank was late again.

Emmy and Micky had been doing the dishes until her father took the tea towel from Micky and shooed them away. Now they sat on the front veranda steps, the twins on either side of them, the front light glowing.

'So,' Jimmy said. 'Are you Emmy's boyfriend now.'

'I would like to be,' Micky replied. Emmy squeezed his hand.

'Have you killed anybody yet?' Jimmy asked, as only an eight-year-old boy could.

Joey leaned across Emmy and said, 'He's a Medic, Medics fix people.'

'Yes, Medics fix people,' Micky repeated. 'I hope I never have to kill anyone,' he told Jimmy.

The front door opened. 'Come inside, boys,' Mama said. 'Let Emmy and Micky alone.'

'Gute Nacht, Frau Cannon,' Micky said

'Gute Nacht, Micky.'

'You speak German?' Emmy said when they were alone.

'No, not really. Simon's grandmother was German, so we learnt some words. Do you?'

'Not much,' she replied. 'Papa insists we speak English. We know some words, like you. I learnt French at school but have forgotten most of it. Papa won't let us speak French at home either, only English.'

'Have your parents been here long?'

'Twenty years. We were born here after they fled Europe. It's something they don't talk about.'

'No,' he said.

'Am I your boyfriend now, Emmaline Marie Cannon?' Micky said.

'I would like that, Michael Brannigan,' she replied.

Chapter Seven

Emmaline

Emmy worked the next three days. Micky met her after work in the city at Aherns; they ate at the Wellington Hotel on Friday night, and on Saturday night, they danced at the Windsor Nightclub on Hay Street. She still wasn't old enough to accompany him, but no one seemed to mind. They swam in the ocean on Sunday morning and took the twins to the Zoo in the afternoon.

On Monday 16th December, Emmy worked and Micky visited his mother's friend. After lunch, he borrowed a car and drove out to York, where he stayed for two nights visiting his mother's brother and sister and his cousins. Emmy couldn't believe how long those two days were.

On Wednesday, Emmy didn't have to work, so Micky picked her up in a taxi, and they shopped, had lunch and swam at Cottesloe beach.

At 6 pm, they entered the foyer of the Pier Hotel on Collie Street, Fremantle, an old building in need of refurbishing, but it was clean. Downstairs, there was a public bar for men only. There was also a lounge where dinner was served, and ladies and gentlemen could buy a drink.

Upstairs, there were ten rooms.

Emmy knew why she had said yes to coming here.

In one of those rooms, Micky pushed the straps of her dress off her shoulders and let it fall to the floor. Emmy fumbled with his buttons and removed his shirt. He took her face in his hands and kissed her mouth, his body hard against hers. When he reached around her back to unclasp her bra, she pushed him away. He looked confused like she was taking a favourite toy away.

'Here,' Emmy said and put his hands to the clasp on the front of her bra. He opened the clip, pushed the fabric away, then cupped her breasts in his hands.

Emmy's legs felt shaky, and she rested her head on Micky's chest; he soon scooped her up, carried her to the bed and lay beside her. She trembled.

'Are you sure?' Micky asked.

'I'm sure,' Emmy said. She was indeed here with Micky because she wanted to be.

Micky

Micky opened his eyes and turned onto his back as the last of the daylight shone through the thin curtains. Emmy rolled onto her back and turned her head to him; he caressed her cheek.

'Hi,' he said.

'Hi.'

'Okay?'

'I've never done that before,' she said.

He knew that. She had trembled in his arms as he lay beside her, and he'd asked her once more, 'Are you sure?'

She had nodded, her hand shaking as she ran her fingers around his chest. He'd covered it with his and guided her, helping her discover his body, and with her permission, he'd discovered hers.

Emmy was a virgin, that wasn't a surprise. What had surprised him was his reaction to it. Emmy had been asleep curled in his arms; he hadn't realised until he'd pushed her hair from his face; it was wet, wet from his tears.

'I hope I didn't hurt you,' he said. He couldn't bear that

thought; he might have hurt her.

He remembered 'the talk' with his father. 'You're a big boy, Micky; always be kind, be gentle. Know what your intentions are and make sure the girl knows what they are. Be respectful, if she says no, that is what she means.' He'd been fourteen.

'You didn't hurt me,' Emmy said. She leant over him, her hair falling onto his face; she pushed it back and he ran his fingers down her cheek.

'My mother never told me anything. No one ever … I never knew …' Tears welled in her eyes. 'I'm glad it was you, Micky … I waited for you,' she said.

He was glad too. He never thought it was important; he'd slept with women before, but he'd never been the first man with anyone. Emmy had waited for him.

'I love you, Emmy,' he said.

He *had* used those words before. You did, when you thought you might love someone, when they told you they loved you and there was nothing else you could say. But this time he knew what he was saying. This time when he said those words, they were right, that he should be saying them. This time he didn't *think* he loved Emmy. He knew.

'Micky, I love you too.'

'What are we going to do?' he asked.

'I don't know.'

She put her arms around his neck, and they made love again.

Emmy lay sleeping beside him. He was leaving next week. He couldn't do anything about it. His mother had made him promise not to leave a girl behind, waiting. He wasn't keeping that promise. Emmy had her life planned out before her and he was going to Vietnam. He wouldn't be fighting in the jungle; he wouldn't be in danger. He pushed the tangled hair from her face and she stirred.

'What time is it?' she asked.

The streetlight now shone in the window: guests were not allowed in the rooms after 10.00 pm. He checked the Rolex on the side table. 'It's after ten.'

Micky and Emmy crept down the stairs, shoes in hands, the only patrons in the hotel.

'Young man!' a female voice said from behind the bar.

'Busted!' Emmy whispered.

'Yes, ma'am.' He turned towards the elderly lady wiping glasses with a towel in the semi-dark.

'Do I know you, young man?' she asked.

'No, ma'am.'

'Are you sure? You look very familiar.'

'Not me, ma'am. My father was billeted here during the war,' he replied.

She came out from behind the bar, looked him up and down then stared at Emmy. 'Yes,' she said. 'He died in the war. I'm sorry.'

'No, ma'am. He was injured, but he survived.'

'I'm happy to hear that,' she said.

'Go on, get out of here.' She flicked her tea towel at them as she sent them on their way.

As Micky opened the door, he heard her say: 'Your father never took any notice of the signs I put at the bottom of the stairs either.'

Chapter Eight

Emmaline

Two days later Emmy and Julie hurried out the front door of Aherns on Hay Street. They laughed and giggled on their way home after a busy day at work.

'Emmaline!' Emmy heard her name; she wasn't expecting Micky to meet her after work and turned, excited to see him. He was dressed in his white uniform, his kit bag lying on the ground at his feet.

Julie said, 'I'll see you tomorrow.'

'Mmm, yes, tomorrow,' Emmy said. *Micky's in his uniform.* 'Micky?' She couldn't move. When he took hold of her hands, she could see the tears in his eyes.

'I have to go.'

'Go?'

'I received a cable. The Jackson is leaving Singapore tomorrow. I have a flight out tonight. I'm sorry. Come to the airport with me.'

She nodded.

The taxi ride to the airport just happened – they were there before she knew it. And now she stood on the tarmac, a Qantas plane ready to tear her life apart.

Micky wrapped his arm around her, the noise from the plane engines growing louder as they moved towards the steps. She didn't want to move towards it. If she didn't move, it would all go away. She should have had time, time to *think about it tomorrow*, like Scarlet O'Hara in Gone with the Wind.

They were at the bottom of the steps: he had to board. But he stepped out of the queue and took her face in his hands.

'Wait for me, Emmaline, please. Will you wait for me?' Micky asked.

'Yes … I … I love you, Micky. I will wait for you … I will wait for you forever.'

'I love you, Emmy. I will come back. Write to me, visit my grandfather. My father was right, I knew the first time I saw you I didn't need to ask that question.'

He reached around the back of his neck, undid a clasp and took a gold chain with a heart-shaped locket from where it hung.

'My father gave this to my mother when he left her in the war. Wear it for me, look after it for me. I will get it when I come back. I promise.' He put the chain around her neck and tightened the clasp.

Emmy rested her head on his chest. Then Micky lifted her chin, took her face in his hands and kissed her mouth. He had to go; she had to let him go. He pulled out of her arms, and she stood, her arms by her side, watching him walk up the stairs.

At the top, he turned and touched his hat. She didn't cry. *Mustn't let him see tears; tears will wait.*

She clung to his promise … tomorrow's promise. *He will come back.*

He was the last passenger to board the plane, and after he entered the cabin, the doors shut. Emmy stood alone. The noise from the engines should have hurt her ears, but she felt nothing.

She turned the gold locket over in her hands. It was very old and inscribed on the back was one word.

'Forever.'

Chapter Nine

January 1969

Micky

New Year's Eve on a navy vessel is celebrated like anywhere else on the planet unless you are on duty.

On New Year's Day 1969, Micky, Simon and William stood leaning over the ship's railing as it made its way into the harbour at Da Nang. The wind blew their cobwebs away as land came into focus.

Micky couldn't believe how beautiful it was. Golden sands, azure sea and green forests growing to the water's edge until you turned the other way. The golden sands were covered with army tents, men and machinery. Helicopters flew overhead, the thump, thump, thump of their blades joining the choir of noise.

The *Jackson* pulled into dock, and the task of disembarking troops and equipment destined for the battlefield began. Micky, Simon and William were seconded to the 95th Evacuation Hospital for the next twelve months.

His buddies had teased him mercilessly when he'd joined the ship in Singapore. He was in love, and it showed; he was like a schoolboy bubbling over and couldn't hide it. He didn't try. He'd thought he had more time with Emmy, but having to leave in a hurry helped saying goodbye. There had been no time to think about it. It had just happened.

He had written to his mother.

Dear Mum,

His mother had never liked the use of the word 'mother' when he addressed her.

I've met the girl I want to spend my life with.

Mum, I can't put into words how Emmaline makes me feel. I feel like I'm whole with her in my life. I know that sounds silly because I wasn't unhappy before I met her. I know you will love her, and I know you will understand and forgive me for falling in love with her and leaving her behind. I understand what you meant now.

Emmy has promised to wait for me and I'm sure I will be safe at the medical post, and we will be together soon.

I love you,

Micky

Two weeks later, any little boy notion he'd had of war being a noble pursuit was gone. He was still proud of who he was and what he did, even more so. He'd attended injured sailors before, the result of accidents and carelessness, even the result of friendly fire, as they called it, but he'd never seen what an IED could do; never seen what happens to a man when he treads on a mine. Now he knew.

Simon's body trembled, the cigarette in his hand not quite alight. He offered Micky a drag. He'd never smoked; he'd never wanted to, but he took the cigarette with a shaking hand, took a deep breath in, then handed it back to Simon.

They sat on a bench outside the hospital, covered in blood. It was four in the afternoon, humid and sticky, flies buzzing around, and they'd been on duty since six that morning. It was now quiet.

A shadow fell over them, and they went to stand. 'As you were,' the instruction came. Major Smith, head surgeon, took the cigarette Simon offered and shared his for a light.

'We have to do our best,' he said. 'We can't let them die.' He sat beside them.

Why not? Micky wanted to say. The soldier was screaming, crying that he wanted to die; he didn't want to live. His legs were gone, his face blown apart.

In the quiet between helicopters, the truth was hard. They had to do their best. They had to save the life – that was what they were there for. The major shared a cigarette and the quiet before leaving them on their own.

Time to get cleaned up. Half the night would be spent patrolling the grounds before a few hours' sleep, and then it was back to the wards. As he rose from the bench, Simon grabbed his arm and said, 'Don't send me back to Becky like that. Please don't send me back like that.'

Micky took his arm and said, 'I won't.'

Mail was being delivered. Micky heard his name called.

He'd been in Vietnam almost four weeks, and this was his first letter from Emmy. He took the envelope into his tent, eager to read, but there was the sound … the thump, thump, thump of helicopter blades. He knew how to tell the difference between helicopters now: this one was bringing wounded. He wouldn't have time to read his letter, so he put it on his bunk and ran out to meet the incoming aircraft.

Five hours later, Micky ducked his head, his ears throbbed, echoing the relentless explosions surrounding him. He flicked the ash floating down on him away, pulled the cloth covering his mouth up. Dirt filled air hurt his lungs, he was covered in sweat and mud and he had his blood on his uniform. *A hospital should be safe from enemy attack*, ran through his mind, but ambulances were lining up and the wounded were being driven away to safety. The hospital was almost empty, Micky returning to help Simon move one more patient. The bombing had grown more accurate – they didn't have much time left before it would be right on top of them. Dust and debris already flew around. He covered the face of the soldier to protect it, took his end of the stretcher and carried the patient out to the waiting ambulance. The ambulance sped away, the hospital now cleared of the wounded. It was time to leave.

My letter! He looked, but his quarters were blown to bits.

'Come on, you two,' William called from the waiting jeep.

'Come on, Micky!' he heard Simon.

Then he heard nothing. The world around him was falling to pieces. Someone pushed him in the back, and he fell into a dark well.

Emmy!

23rd February 1969

> *95th Evacuation Hospital*
> *Da Nang, Vietnam.*

Dear Captain and Mrs Brannigan,

It is my sad duty to inform you that your son, Michael Francis Brannigan, is missing.

Our medical outpost in Da Nang was overrun by the Viet Cong on January 25th. Your son and two other medics managed to evacuate most of the patients in the unit before we were overrun. When we were able to return to the outpost there was no sign of your son.

His heroic actions against such odds saved many lives. You can be proud of this.

Your country is forever in your debt.

Major John Alexander Smith.
United States Army, Surgical Service.

Chapter Ten

May 1969

Emmaline

In the middle of May, Emmy sat on the front step of the workers'
cottage, her two little boys beside her. The veranda light, a single
bulb, lit some of her face. Joey shivered and she put her arm
around him.

'Why do you have to go?' he asked.

'It's where I live now, you know that. I have to go, so the
children can go to school.'

'When will you be home?'

'Not too long. I'm going away for the next school holidays,
but I will be back before Christmas. Anyway, you have my room
now. Where will I sleep if I come back here to live?'

'Yes, we don't have to share with Hank anymore … he smells,'
Jimmy said.

Emmy ruffed his hair. 'All boys smell when they get older.'

'Not us,' Jimmy said.

'When you are older, you will. And then when you are older
again, you won't,' she said.

'Yuk,' they said together.

'Time for bed, boys.' Her father opened the door. 'Say
goodbye to Emmy. She will be gone before you get up
tomorrow.'

'Goodbye, Emmy,' they said.

She wrapped them in her arms and held them tight, breathing

in their scent and trying not to cry. Her father shut the front door and sat on the step beside her.

'Where are you going, Emmaline?'

Emmaline? He never called her that.

She wasn't going back to Wagin, a small country town where the whispers were already going around. She'd been so excited about starting her new life and being in love with Micky.

Late in January, she should have guessed; she should have been more worldly, but she wasn't. By the time February came around, she was being ill in the morning, and she knew. She wasn't unhappy … Micky's baby … how could she be unhappy. She was waiting for his letters.

She wasn't allowed to be happy. Unmarried, the doctor had done the necessary tests; the receptionist and nurse whispered behind their hands.

She looked into her father's face. There was no point in lying. 'I'm going to Melbourne, Papa.'

He put his arm around her shoulder.

'I wanted you to have more, Emmy. I wanted you to have everything your mother couldn't. You were so young when the twins were born. I know how much you missed so you could help me with them.'

'It was okay, Papa. I love my brothers, my boys.' She stared across the dark front lawn.

'You don't have to go away. Stay here, I will look after you.'

'No, Papa. Mama has never gotten over having the twins. It would be too hard for her if I stayed.'

She needed to know after all this time … now she was going to do this, she needed to know. 'What happened to Mama, Papa?'

He'd never spoken about the life they lived before they fled Europe; she could see him thinking.

He said, 'At the end of the war, the Russians captured Berlin. Mama was young, not much older than you. I hadn't met her yet.

The Russians were brutal. They showed no mercy to the residents, especially the women.'

He didn't need to say anymore. Emmy knew what he was telling her. She took his hand.

'She was very fragile when I met her not long after. I was in the French Occupation forces. We fell in love.' He smiled. And Emmy understood.

'Berlin was a pile of rubble; there wasn't a building left undamaged. The women worked as hard as the men. There was no food, and as winter came, no coal for the fires. Her brothers died in the war and her sisters and parents wanted nothing to do with me. I was able to get extra food but still they forbade her from seeing me. We married in secret early in 1946. When I transferred back to France and left the army, she came with me. My family wanted nothing to do with her and turned us out. I found work, and we managed to get a room in Paris. Mama was pregnant.'

'Papa!'

Emmy didn't know any of this. She thought she was the oldest.

'No, Emmy. You had an older brother, but he didn't survive.'

Now she knew.

'We came to Australia to make a new life away from all the destruction and hatred. We are happy here and when you were born, I thought Mama was going to get better. You were a girl and even though you looked like her she was okay. Hank came along, he had dark hair and olive skin, like me. Mama was okay and things seemed good. But having the twins, they were too much like the baby who died; it was too hard for her. You know that.'

'Yes.' Emmy remembered.

She was twelve years old. Papa had to work; Jacob's grandmother helped when she could. There was talk about the

twins going into care, but her father refused to let it happen. He
fought with government agencies, and with the help of one nurse
who supported him, who stood up for him, who listened to
Emmy when she begged and said she would still go to school,
they were allowed to keep them at home.

Mama was in a special hospital. Emmy didn't understand the
words she heard: 'electric shock treatment', 'mental breakdown',
but at twelve, she remembered them and would know what they
meant later.

Mama would come home for visits and, by the time Emmy
was fourteen, she was back living at home. Mama would never
be the same; she would never be the mother and companion to
Emmy she had been before the twins were born.

'Yes, Papa. I remember. So I know I have to leave.'

'What will you do?'

'Father Kelly has arranged a place for me at a home in
Melbourne.'

'Father Kelly?' her father asked. He wasn't their parish priest.

'Father Kelly's from Saint Patrick's in Fremantle. He has been
a great help to me. No one in our church knows anything.'

'That's not important, Emmy,' he said.

'Maybe not. I don't know anymore.' And she didn't care
anymore; she just wanted to get away.

'I will be back at Christmas.'

'And the baby,' he said.

'It will be adopted.' She said the words. That made it real.
Somewhere in the back of her mind, she thought there might be
a knight in shining armour riding to her rescue, but there wasn't.
She had to look after herself.

'You don't have to do that,' her father said.

'I do, Papa. There is no other way.'

He would know who the father was, and she thanked him
silently for not asking the question.

The next day, early in the morning before the sun was up, Jacob opened the back door and took her bags to her father's car. He wanted to drive her back to Wagin, but she'd insisted she would take the bus. The sun rose slowly as they arrived at the bus depot. Emmy stamped her feet to keep warm.

'Thank you,' she said.

She wanted to put her arms around him and thank him. Her thick duffle coat over her long floral skirt should hide her secret. At least now she could dress how she wanted. Her headmaster had pulled her into his office on the first day she had met him and said, 'You will not be wearing any of those hippie style clothing while you are teaching in my school.'

Emmy had her work clothes for when the children were at school, but they hadn't been there that day.

'Is everything okay, Emmy?' Jacob asked.

'Of course.' She put her arms around him. 'I'm fine. I always miss the boys when I leave them.'

'Will you be back for the Public holiday in June?'

'No, it's only one day. It would be too hard to arrange.'

'I can pick you up.'

'No, Jacob. You have to look after your grandmother.'

'Yes.'

'I hope she gets better,' Emmy said. 'I will see you soon.'

Jacob walked back to the parked car. The bus for Wagin pulled into the depot, and he turned to make sure she was on the bus then drove away. Emmy had left her case on the ground next to the bus – thankfully Jacob hadn't noticed – and she clambered out of her seat and hurried down the bus steps.

'Come on miss,' the driver said. 'Let's put your case away so we can head out.'

'I'm sorry … I'm on the wrong bus,' Emmy said. She picked up her case and headed across to the bus stand marked Melbourne.

The sun inched its way into the sky as the bus drove out of the city, through the town of Midland on the way to Emmy's new life. Three days on a bus, five months pregnant, with a little money she'd saved up, and Papa had given her $200.00 from his savings.

Father Kelly had arranged for her to stay at St Joseph's, a home for unwed expecting mothers, where she could keep her baby while she made her final decision.

Emmy could not terminate the child; Father Kelly had known. She could not keep the child either, for she could not bring a child into her family's home. Even if Mama could manage, there would be too much shame, too many questions asked, too much for her brothers to share.

Perhaps one day being an unmarried mother would not be scorned by society; one day, there would be more support; one day, there might be more options for girls like her.

Emmy hoped the child would understand. She could only give it life and dream that its life would be full of love, that the child would be cherished and provided for and have a life Emmy could not give it. Then she would pretend none of this had happened.

Emmy had loved Michael Brannigan; she did love Michael Brannigan. But she would keep her heart closed from now on. She never wanted to love like that again; it was too much to lose. She would never know what had happened to Micky; she couldn't believe he had left her: she wanted to believe it. But she was on her own as she looked out the window of the Greyhound bus as the town of Northam flew by.

Chapter Eleven

Emmaline

In July, Emmy sat in the living room of the home she shared in Melbourne, keeping very much to herself. Her lifelong friends, girls she had grown up with, had disappeared like she was contagious when they'd found out she was pregnant, making her wary of friendships now.

On a black and white television, Emmy watched a man walk on the moon.

The news reports also showed the cost of a war far away. Violent protests, nations tearing themselves apart as the people saw the deaths and losses they were incurring. The news reports showed bags with bodies loaded into helicopters, coffins draped in flags placed with dignity and care onto aircraft. And she prayed. She prayed Micky wasn't in one of those bags because of all the things that could have happened to him that was the one she would never recover from.

But who will tell me? How will I know? Emmy clutched the gold locket hanging around her neck. His promise.

On September 1st, 1969, Emmy turned twenty-one. She could vote and legally drink alcohol. She could also make all her own decisions, decisions she had already made.

Two weeks later, her body was being torn apart as her child tried to force its way into the world. She was in a room – a ward maybe – she would never know, her only source of privacy a drawn curtain. Her fear was compounded by the terror she could hear around her; she wasn't the only one delivering a child into the world.

'Why hasn't this girl been given any Entonox?' Emmy heard the words like they were far away.

It seemed like she'd been in this room for days, her lips were dry and chaffed, her hair damp and limp, her body covered in sweat. She felt dirty and ashamed. Emmy tried not to cry out, tried not to make a fuss, but every contraction was more painful than the one before, closer than the one before.

'She shouldn't need it.' Emmy heard the reply.

Emmy waited, waited for the next contraction, which she knew wouldn't be long. She tried to regain her breath, tried to regain some control. As the next contraction began, a mask was placed over her face. She pushed it away.

'It's alright, Emmaline. This will help. Breathe in with the pain.' Emmy's eyes rested on Sister Mary-Anne as she held the mask over her face.

'Gently now,' Sister Mary-Anne said.

The next voice she heard was male.

'How long has this been?'

'Since yesterday around lunchtime, the other woman in the room, Sister Ursula, said.

Sister Mary-Anne removed the mask and said, 'The doctor's here now, Emmaline. It won't be long now, then you will need to push.'

Emmy felt tired. She wanted to leave; she wanted this all to be over. She felt like her life had come down to this day, in this bed, behind these curtains with so much pain and noise around her. 'I can't,' she said.

'Yes, you can. Baby needs you,' Sister Mary-Anne said. She held Emmy's hand as the pain of childbirth surrounded her. 'Push now, Emmaline.'

Emmy did. Gathering all her strength, she pushed with the

pain, then as it subsided, Sister Mary-Anne said, 'Rest now.'

'Why wasn't I called earlier. What is her name?' the male voice asked.

'Emmaline,' Sister Mary-Anne replied.

'It won't be long now, Emmaline,' he said. 'I need you to do exactly as I say. Can you?'

Emmy tried to nod.

Sister Mary-Anne held her hand as the doctor helped her child into the world. Metal instruments, intrusions into her body, lights in her eyes, Emmy pushed her torn and exhausted body until she was unable to push anymore. She heard the child cry as it came into the world.

Sister Mary-Anne wrapped the child in a cloth and said, 'A girl, Emmaline. A beautiful baby girl.'

'Is she okay?' Emmy murmured.

'Perfect. She's perfect. Would you like to hold her?'

Emmy turned her head away; she could not stop the tears that ran down her cheeks.

'No, please. I don't want to see her.'

She would never be able to do what she had to if she did.

Chapter Twelve

December 1969

Emmaline.

Three o'clock in the afternoon and already it was getting dark. It wasn't supposed to be like this. London, the centre of the universe. London, the swinging sixties, nearly the seventies, where all the music and fashion came from, where a bedsit in Earls Court seemed like a good place to hide.

Emmy had always wanted to go to London. She'd always planned to save her money and go there one day. She didn't have to save her money – it had arrived one day from Father Kelly, a bequest from a wealthy couple, a donation to the church.

Emmy didn't want to remember what had happened to her when her baby was born. A blur of drugs and pain, the baby taken away without Emmy seeing her. That was what she wanted, better that way, no attachments, but Emmy's body cried out for the child it had made.

The child was to be adopted, until the day she was placed in Emmy's arms. When Sister Mary-Anne asked her, 'Would you like to see your baby?' Emmy had always said, 'No,' but this time she had said, 'Yes.'

Her little girl was a week old, without a name, alone in a crib in a nursery, her hair dark and curly, her eyes already going brown. *So like Micky.* Her little face was bruised by the metal instruments that had helped her into the world.

Sister Mary-Anne had picked her out of the crib and placed

her in Emmy's arms, where she sat in a wheelchair. Emmy knew she would never leave her again and whispered to the child, 'I'm here. Your Mama's here.'

Emmy had given her child a name, Mia, something like her father's. She had been reluctant to take the money; she would not have taken it if she hadn't met Mia, but she did. Emmy took Mia, the money and left.

It wasn't quite that simple though. It had taken time for her body to recover. Then she had to learn to feed her baby, and she understood why Father Kelly had sent her to St Joseph's, because it was there she had time.

Emmy put the cheque in the bank and arranged for the passports and airfares for herself and her baby. She was only able to do this because of a wealthy couple she had never met, who would never meet her, who she could never repay.

Emmy hadn't thought it through; she discovered it almost immediately when she arrived in London. She could work, of course – she was a teacher – but she would do anything. She had a baby; she knew how to look after a baby: she'd looked after her brothers when they were born. But she was on her own in London and babies don't sleep, food was expensive, and it was cold.

She'd been able to bluff her way into the bedsit. Although she didn't think the owner believed her story about her husband coming from Australia soon, he'd let her the property anyway. Three months' rent in advance and no questions asked. A room to sleep in with a kitchenette in one corner, a chair to sit in front of the fire if you had the coins for the heater. Hot and cold water taps in the kitchen. Her own toilet. But she shared the bathroom on the landing – she was the only one who used it every day.

Baby's nappies she soaked and hung inside, after her first attempt at hanging them in the shared garden. On a bright winter's day in Perth, you would put the laundry out. Not in

London: the laundry was as stiff as cardboard and frozen solid when she went to bring it in, she learnt. Clothing was then washed and dried in a laundry in Earls Court Square.

Oxfam shops were good for essentials for her and Mia. She became the Queen of Pine-o-clean, scrubbing everything she bought for Mia until her hands hurt and no germs could survive.

Twice a week, she would have a real cup of coffee; she would bundle Mia up in her pram and walk around the corner to Old Brompton Road. The café served real coffee, not instant powdered coffee, and on a sunny day, she could sit in the garden and read or listen to music. The shop reminded her of Luigi's, the smell of ground coffee and pastries, so she felt a little less homesick when she was there. Emmy had the offer of a few hours of work in the café, doing the dishes, which helped pay for her coffee. Mia would sleep in her pram in a corner within her sight while she did this; no one objected. Mia seemed to enjoy the attention she received from the people at the café.

Emmy had promised the twins she would be home for Christmas, but she wasn't. She'd spent a little of her money on gifts for them – a Matchbox police car for Jimmy and a red double-decker bus for Joey – and wrote them a card, telling them she was on a big adventure, that she'd gone to London to visit the Queen, like the Pussy Cat in the nursery rhyme. She had included a postcard for her parents, telling them she was well and having the time of her life enjoying the excitement of living in London. She didn't tell them about Mia. Lying in a letter was easy.

She never put her address on the envelope, had her mail sent Post Restante, saying it was best as she was moving around a lot. She wasn't ready to tell them the truth and wondered if she ever could. Papa would understand, but how would it affect Mama?

Christmas day: Emmy cooked an English Christmas Lunch,

or what she thought was an English Christmas lunch. Not a whole turkey for her but a piece and roast potatoes, carrots, peas, gravy, cranberry sauce. She had a Christmas cake from Andrea, who ran the café, and Mia had a little tree with gifts from Emmy and Andrea under it. It was her first Christmas, and she was just over three months old.

It wasn't a white Christmas, but it was cold. Emmy rugged up and pushed Mia around the heath after she'd stuffed herself silly. Many people wandered the heath full of Christmas cheer and happiness, so Emmy wasn't so lonely.

On New Year's Eve, Emmy pushed Mia around a cold and damp Trafalgar Square; she was home before five.

Chapter Thirteen

Emmaline

In the middle of January, Emmy received a letter from Jacob saying he was coming to London. He would go to Trafalgar Square on the 20th and wait all day for her. He hadn't seemed surprised when she turned up pushing a pram. He looked at Mia, told her how beautiful she was and didn't ask any more questions. They shared tea, and Emmy ate fish with her chips, this time while Jacob told her his story.

He'd always thought he was German. He looked German, being tall and slim with blond hair and blue eyes. His grandmother spoke German, was German.

'When Oma died, I went through her belongings and found a box of documents, letters and a few old photographs. I also found items of jewellery she had kept hidden. These pieces of jewellery turned out to be valuable,' Jacob told her.

He knew his parents had died in the war not long after he was born, and his grandmother had raised him. That was true. What he didn't know was how his parents had died.

'I found letters in a box, written in German. My parents left Berlin in the mid-thirties and moved to Amsterdam. When the Nazis arrested my father in August 1944, I was out with Oma. My mother fled with my brother and sister,' he told Emmy. 'I have a brother and sister, Emmy. I didn't know that … What happened to my family?'

His grandmother's letters mentioned people she knew in London before she migrated to Australia. There was so much he didn't know or understand, so many secrets.

Emmy held Jacob's hand as he told her. 'I sold some of the jewellery and bought a ticket to London. I knew you were here … I'm glad I found you.'

That was three days ago.

Emmy was cold. Mia, feeding at her breast, was cold. She hadn't known she could be this cold; her face hurt, and her feet; she couldn't get her feet warm no matter how she tried. When she finished feeding, she pulled the blanket around Mia; wrapped her as warm as she could and held her close.

The heater was out; it had been out for an hour. She had a one shilling piece. If she used it on the heater, it would be gone. If she didn't, how cold would they get? How much longer should she wait?

Jacob opened the door.

'For God's sake, Emmy, you can't live this.' He took his coat off and wrapped it around her, took coins from his pocket and fed the heater, turning it up high. He lifted Mia from her arms and carried her closer to the warmth.

'If you won't let me help you, let me help Mia,' he said.

'She's not yours.'

'I know that,' he snapped back at her. He tried to hide his anger from her, but they had grown up together.

'I'm sorry, Jacob.' Emmy rose from the chair, went to the kitchenette, turned on the kettle and made coffee. She put the cups on the coffee table and huddled near the heater. Jacob put Mia into her crib. And the room warmed up.

'Thank you,' Emmy said.

'We can go home if you like,' Jacob said. 'I will say Mia's mine. We can get married.'

Emmy took his hand. Jacob should be with someone who loved him, not her. 'I can't, Jacob. It's not fair; you deserve better.'

'Emmy. You can't stay here on your own. Come with me to Amsterdam then. No one's going to know us; no one's going to care. We can make up a story.'

Another lie. She was getting used to it.

Chapter Fourteen

Emmaline

At the end of March, on a bus to Amsterdam, they looked like a young couple with their baby, and that was what they were going to be.

Before going to the bus depot, Emmy picked up her mail. There was one package: the postmark read Melbourne. Emmy thought it was something she had left behind.

Emmy redirected her future mail to Amsterdam. From now on, it would be addressed to Jacob Miller. Post Restante required a passport to be picked up, so she couldn't lie about that. There wasn't much mail, only letters from Papa.

Mia slept peacefully in Jacob's arms as Emmy opened the package. Inside the package was clothing for a baby. Vests, jumpers, and Bonds baby suits, booties, beanies and a thick blanket, all in white or baby yellow. There was an envelope containing £10 notes, nothing else; no card, no name. Nothing to say who had sent it. Emmy put two of the notes in her purse and tucked the rest into the bottom of her backpack. She placed the blanket over Mia, rested her head on Jacob's shoulder and closed her eyes.

She was warm, and Mia was flourishing, only waking once a night for feeding; she was eating some solid food and slept well in the warm room. Out through the window, Emmy could see a late fall of snow, houses leaning up against each other, covered in white, like a picture book, and canals full of water, some of it frozen. There was snow on the balconies and on the trees. Emmy could see a different beauty. Trees were trying to bud, showing spring was not far away.

They had been in Amsterdam almost four weeks, Jacob having rented a bedsit for them rather than a hotel room. They had their own bathroom, and Emmy was the *little housekeeper* —it was the least she could do for him. Her affection for him hadn't changed; he'd always been in her life, and she loved him, and he knew how she loved him. He never asked for more.

Jacob had searched London for information about his brother and sister. The only clue he had was an address in Amsterdam, but he was not getting very far. The address in Amsterdam no longer existed. When he opened the door, his face showed how his day had been.

Emmy put the coffee on the table and sat opposite him.

'No news today,' he said.

She took his hand.

'I'll have to sell some jewellery tomorrow,' he said.

'I have some money. Let me help.' He had refused to let her put money into the rent, only letting her contribute to the cost of food.

'Let's see what we get first.'

'Jacob.'

The next day Emmy and Jacob tramped the streets of Amsterdam's Diamond district, which was very different to where they lived. Emmy pushed her baby in a pram, her grey and white checked woollen coat worn over a long black skirt with knee-high boots bought from the Oxfam shop. She felt out of place. Jacob, dressed in a suit and a Herringbone coat, looked more like he should be there. They'd been to a couple of jewellery shops to get a price on a ring, for which there was a big difference in the amounts offered. Neither of them knew much about diamonds but Jacob was sure the ring was as valuable as any he'd priced in Perth.

The sun shone in a pale blue, cold sky. Bicycles and trams drove past as they sat at the streetside café. Coffee was shared, Emmy fed Mia and propped her up in the pram. Dressed in her new clothes with her white and yellow blanket tucked around her and a white beanie over her dark curls, she was smiling and gurgling.

'There's another shop around the corner,' Jacob said. 'We'll try there, and then we will decide.'

The shop was old on the outside but refurbished and well lit inside. The name hanging on the hoarding read Goldstein. In the shop, the man behind the counter studied the ring with his eyepiece.

'Where did you get this?' he asked in precise English.

'It was my grandmother's,' Jacob said. 'She passed away last year.'

He examined the ring again. Then he looked Jacob up and down, studying his face.

'I would like to buy this from you. I will give you a good price, but I would like you to bring it back tomorrow.'

Jacob shrugged and looked at Emmy.

'We can come back tomorrow,' Emmy said.

She had her £10 notes and insisted on changing one into the local currency. The rent was paid for another week.

The following day they were back in the shop. This time an old man examined the ring. He spoke to the younger man, who said, 'You said this was your grandmother's ring.'

'Yes,' Jacob answered.

The older man spoke Dutch, and the younger man asked, 'What was her name?'

'My name is Miller. It was the name she used. I think she changed it to Miller when we went to Australia.'

'Australia?' the older man said.

'Yes, we migrated to Australia after the war. We were in London for a little time.'

Jacob stopped talking. The old man had tears running down his face. 'Sofia,' he said.

'Yes,' Jacob said. 'Sofia Miller, my grandmother.'

'Sofia Muller, mijn vriendin,' the old man said.

The younger man helped him to a seat.

Then he said to Jacob, 'My grandfather. I recognised his work when you bought the ring in yesterday. He tells me Sofia was a friend; he helped her and you. Your father was part of the resistance, helping hide Jews in Amsterdam. He was arrested and threatened with execution if he did not reveal the location of the families he was helping,' the younger man said.

He looked at his grandfather and patted him on the shoulder. They spoke quietly in Dutch.

Then he said, 'We are too young to remember, but our parents and grandparents do. Grandfather tells me Sofia was German, like your mother. Your father's father, your grandfather, was Jewish, but he had never practised the faith. You looked German, so they passed you off as Sofia's son, a late surprise. Your mother fled with your brother and sister, I'm sorry.'

Emmy held Jacob's trembling arm.

'What happened to them?' he asked. She could hear the tears in his voice.

'We know your mother died in 1945. We don't know what happened to your brother and sister; their names are not on any lists of the dead. The last we heard was they had been secretly sent to England.'

'I've been there,' Jacob said. 'Those who knew grandmother know nothing of any other children. I don't even know their correct name. The only name I know is Millar, and that can't be right, can it?'

'Many young people went searching for their identity. Some

went to what is now called Israel,' Jacob was told.

Jacob cried in Emmy's bed that night.

Two weeks later, they returned to London.

Jacob had his father's name and the names of his brother and sister on a slip of paper, none of which helped.

At the beginning of June, they took a ship to Israel. The journey would take them over two weeks.

Chapter Fifteen

June 1973

Emmaline

Emmy wandered along the white sands of Cottesloe Beach, where perfect winter waves rolled in and a scattering of board riders enjoyed the space. The name blew past her on the breeze. Not her.

'Emmaline.'

Emmy stumbled. The blue June sky held no warmth, and she shivered, gulped down air. *It can't be. Why did I think I could come home. I should have stayed away, away where it was safe.*

'Emmaline.'

His voice. She hadn't heard his voice for more than four years; had thought she would never hear his voice again. She wanted to run, to get away, but couldn't. Wouldn't. Not from him.

'Emmaline, please. Please wait for me.'

He'd said those words before.

Emmy steadied herself, pulled her duffle coat together, breathed and turned to face him. He struggled across the sand, a stick for support, his dark hair curled near his collar, his navy windbreaker hanging on him.

'Emmaline.'

Pale thin face. Empty brown eyes full of tears, the sparkle was gone from them. A shadow hovering. Micky stood before her.

'Where did you go? My parents looked for you … your father couldn't help them find you,' he said.

Emmy's legs buckled, and she crumpled onto the sand at his feet. Micky lowered himself and sat next to her; put his arm around her, lifted her chin to wipe the tears from her cheeks.

'Where did you go?' she asked.

Why had she thought she could be over him? Swallowing her pain, she dragged in air. *His scent.* After all this time, she remembered his scent, mixed with his cologne containing nutmeg and cinnamon. She could feel his ribs beneath his jacket.

The gold locket fell out of the front of her jumper, and he took it in his hands; looked into her eyes.

'Micky,' Emmy whispered. She took his face in her hands, wiped the tears from his cheeks. She could never be over him.

A shadow fell over them, and a voice said, 'This is Emmaline.'

The speaker was an older version of Micky, a tall man with greying hair, dark eyes and the same smile. *Micky's father.* He reached out and helped her up, and they stood together while Micky struggled to his feet.

'Mama,' said Emmy's daughter, Micky's daughter, nearly four years old, with brown eyes and dark curly hair sitting on her shoulders. She was nothing like her mother and father, which was commented on every time they met anyone new, so much so they had stopped trying to explain.

'Mama, why are you crying?'

Jacob followed her across the sand, and she said to him, 'Papa, why is Mama crying?'

Micky lost his step and took his father's arm for support. He searched her face. She would not hide the truth from him.

'I have to go,' Emmy said.

'I'm okay, Mia. I tripped over, and these kind gentlemen helped me up.'

Emmy took her daughter's hand and said to Micky, 'Thank you for your help.'

She turned, took Jacob's arm, walked away, and would have

fallen if he hadn't been there. He'd done this for her so often, and he knew she could never love him as he deserved.

Micky

Micky's father held him upright. *Four years!* He hadn't seen Emmy for more than four years. Her hair was shorter, darker, and now sat on her shoulders, and her eyes … her eyes … had lost their little girl innocence. Yet she still wore the gold locket he had given her.

Her fingers on his cheeks, he remembered her touch; he had waited so long for her touch. Breathing hurt; being alive hurt. Emmy had walked away from him holding another man's arm, his child with her. She was *his* child. Mia. Emmy called her Mia.

When he could no longer see Emmy, he let his father help him up the grassed embankment where they found a seat.

Four years. An eternity. She didn't know where I'd been. How could she? He dropped his head into his hands and cried the tears he hadn't been able to cry all those years. His father put his arm around his shoulders. He was once again that little boy who'd tried to do something he wasn't old enough to do and had come unstuck. He let himself be that little boy.

His father said, 'Come on now, your mother's waiting.'

His mother had thought him dead; thought she had lost him. Then one day, she had received a letter meant for him, Emmy's letter telling him she was pregnant, saying she hoped he would be happy with the news. A letter he'd never received; a letter that had gone back to Emmy unopened before it was posted on to his mother. He had promised Emmy he would come back, but her letter to him had been returned to her unopened.

Yet Emmy still wore the locket he'd given her.

Chapter Sixteen

Emmaline

Emmy knocked on the door as a taxi pulled up at the front gate. The door opened, and Micky's father stood before her, dressed in a dark naval uniform.

'I was hoping you would be here, Mr Brannigan,' Emmy said.

'My name is Michael. Call me Michael,' he said.

Emmy nodded.

Then a woman came to the door. She wore a long royal blue gown with lace overlaid on the bodice, her dark hair bundled on top of her head, the streaks of grey adding highlights. Her blue eyes opened wider on seeing Emmy.

'Kate, this is Emmaline,' Michael said.

Emmy didn't know what to do. *Should I shake hands?* But she simply nodded again and stood there. The woman held out her arms and said, 'May I?'

Emmy fell into her embrace.

'Micky's out the back,' his father said. 'Come on, we will be late.' He smiled at Emmy. 'Can't keep the Ambassador waiting.'

He took Kate's hand and Emmy watched them walk down the pathway into the waiting taxi. She heaved in a breath, walked down the hallway, through the kitchen and opened the back door.

Micky said, 'Have a good time,' before he turned and saw her standing there.

Emmy stood in the doorway, her denim flares and paisley shirt not keeping her warm. She pulled the front of her navy cardigan together, but that didn't help.

'Your husband lets you visit other men …' he said.

If he'd been angry, upset or bitter Emmy could have handled that, but there was nothing in his words.

'He's not my husband,' she said and sat on the top step beside him.

'Mia called him Papa.'

'It's easier.'

The light coming through the kitchen window showed his face as he stared out into the darkness, into the backyard.

'Does she know about me?'

'Not yet.'

'Do you sleep with him?' he asked.

'Sometimes … sort of.'

Those words should have hurt. Emmy thought they might, but they sat there between them, not angry, not a surprise, just sitting there. He turned to face her.

'What does that mean?'

'I don't love Jacob,' Emmy said.

'*Like that*,' he said. His eyes looked empty, his face blank.

'I never lied to him. I don't think he loves me *like that*, he just thinks he should. He knows he's not you,' she said. 'He deserves better.'

Emmy reached out to his face, but he pulled away.

'I owe him …'

Emmy looked Micky in the eyes and said, 'We owe him a lot, Micky.'

'Why didn't you go to my grandfather. My parents would have helped you,' he said.

'My letters … weren't opened, Micky.'

'What about your parents? Your mother?'

'I couldn't, Micky. Mama couldn't even look after the twins when they were born.'

He put his hand on top of her hand, and she folded her other one over it. Four years slipped away. She had been young, full of dreams and idealism. And alone.

'I'm sorry,' Micky said.

Emmy caressed Micky's hand. 'Do you want to tell me?' he asked. She took a breath and said, 'It was a surprise – I was so naïve. We all thought you couldn't get pregnant the first time. I was stupid.'

'No, Emmy,' he said.

'But I was happy, Micky. I loved you. I believed you and, even though it wasn't what I'd planned, I thought we would be together; we would be happy.'

'We would …' He turned his face away from her.

She reached out and touched his face, turning it to look at her. His eyes, full of shadows, locked with hers. She was foolish to think she could get over him no matter how hard she tried. She would never get over Micky.

'I always loved you, Emmaline. I will always love you,' he said.

He rubbed her arms. 'You're cold,' he said. 'Come inside. I'll make a cup of tea. Or you can have coffee if you like.' A quiet, almost fearful smile crossed his face.

Micky pulled himself up from the step and took up his walking stick. Emmy stood beside him and gave him the dignity of looking after himself.

Micky

In the kitchen, Micky rested his stick on the kitchen wall. He put wood in the old stove and stirred up the flame to warm the room of his grandfather's house, now the home his family used when they visited Australia. Then he turned on the electric kettle. He hadn't been able to go to his grandfather's funeral. After more than sixty years together, it was said he died of a broken heart. He might have scoffed at that before he met Emmy.

He had never received Emmy's letters, but she was the sole reason he survived. Endless pain, loneliness and darkness, looking after each other, trying to keep each other alive. He'd failed. It wasn't his fault, he'd been told, but he had failed.

'Do you want to tell me?' Emmy asked.

'Not yet,' he said.

He put the teapot and cups on the table, sat on the chair opposite her and poured the tea. Emmy warmed her hands on the cup as she sipped the liquid.

'Tell me about Mia?' he asked.

'She looks like you, Micky. Every time I look at her, I see you. I couldn't understand what would have kept you away. I prayed you weren't dead. But I wouldn't know … no one knew about me.

'Grandpa did.'

'Yes, I know. I was afraid. When my letters came back unopened, I could only think you didn't want me.'

'Emmy.' He reached for her hand, and she gave it to him.

He said, 'One of your letters reached my parents.'

'How?'

'Frank Kelly posted it on. You left it in his home.'

'The priest?' Emmy looked at his hand holding hers.

'He's a close family friend.'

'What did he tell you?'

'Nothing, Emmy. He posted the letter on. My mother never expected him to break any confidences. She received the letter in May, the letter telling me you were pregnant. My parents came to Australia looking for you. Your father couldn't tell them anything other than you had gone to Melbourne, that Frank Kelly had arranged a place for you in a home. You always had your mail delivered to the post office, so your father had no address.'

'I was afraid, Micky. Father Kelly was kind to me and helped me when I needed it.'

Micky caressed her lips with his fingers. Then he said, 'My parents knew Frank would know where you were, but they didn't ask. They tried to provide for you. They searched all the homes in Melbourne but couldn't find you. In November, they returned to Melbourne to try again. One day, at one of the homes, a Sister they were speaking to hinted about a girl with your name going to London. Nothing else. Nothing about the baby. My mother hoped you would keep our baby. She sent packages to post offices in London. All went back to her, except one.'

'Father Kelly never said anything about you, Micky,' she said.

'He would not have tried to influence you,' Micky said. 'He is a good man.'

Emmaline

Father Kelly. Emmy had wandered the streets of Fremantle alone and pregnant on a day that had turned cold and wet. She had found herself at Saint Patrick's church on Adelaide Street. Her childhood upbringing, her religion sitting in her mind, she had sought comfort inside but there was no comfort in the cold, empty building. She had found warmth and comfort in the home of Father Kelly.

He had written to her after that visit, taken her address from the back of the letter she had left behind and had asked her to meet him.

I can arrange accommodation for you close to home or far away if you want, he'd written.

When she came home three weeks later for the Anzac Day weekend, she'd gone to see him. He never mentioned her last visit other than to enquire how she was since he'd seen her. But he would have known who the father of her child was. His name was on the front of the letter she'd left there.

Things now began to make sense.

'The place he arranged for me wasn't what I'd expected,'

Emmy said. 'I thought I would be condemned, and I was by some, but most of the sisters were kind enough, doing what they had to. I wasn't the only one there, of course. We worked and some of the girls lived there with their babies; it gave us time to decide. Most of the babies were adopted in the end. The girls didn't have a choice, but it was nice to think we might for a little time.'

Micky's face was blank as she told him.

'He sent me money, Micky. A little donation, he wrote, and it was okay – I needed it. Money doesn't last long if you are not earning anymore.

'One day, he sent me a cheque drawn on a bank – it was for more money than I would have earned in a year. I sent it back to him. He sent it back to me, saying it was from a wealthy benefactor who was making donations to the church, especially for girls in my situation. Not quite a lie, I guess.'

Micky poured more tea. Emmy took the cup and blew on the steaming liquid.

'I wasn't going to spend the money, Micky. After Mia was born, I never saw her; she was taken away. I didn't know what to do. I couldn't bring her home, and I hoped she'd be better off without me. But your body doesn't know you haven't got a baby to feed.'

Emmy pushed her tears back; wiped under her eyes with the back of her fingers.

'I'm sorry, Emmy. I'm sorry you had to go through that. I should have ...' he said. Tears rolled down his cheeks.

'Father Kelly must have understood. He knew who you were, knew you loved me, knew I loved you; I could not give our child away.'

Micky pushed himself from the chair; limped around to where she sat and, lifting her from the chair, he took her in his arms. He ran his fingers through her hair and closed his eyes as he kissed her lips.

Remembering everything they had shared together, she curled into his chest. She was in Micky's arms again.

In the bedroom, Emmy unbuttoned Micky's checked flannel shirt. And stopped breathing.

'Micky,' she whispered.

He lowered his eyes.

'It's okay,' he said.

Emmy tilted his head so he looked into her eyes.

'It's not okay,' she said. *How could this be okay?*

She was afraid to touch him for fear of hurting him. The light from the bedroom lamp showed his body, showed burn marks and welts, some old, some not so old. Evidence of so much violence, so much hatred, so much pain. The ribs she had felt through his jacket glared at her.

He took her hands and placed them on a puckered and raised scar running down his chest to his denim jeans. She traced the line with her finger, and he shuddered when she did. She ran her hands around his precious body then pressed her lips to the scar. He was unsteady on his feet, and she helped him to the bed and lay down beside him.

Emmy was dreaming. She could hear an animal howling, the howling getting louder, closer. Then she was awake. Micky was screaming beside her, and thrashing about the bed.

'Micky,' she called. 'Wake up, Micky!'

He lashed out, striking her face. He threw his arms over her, grabbed her by the wrists, and held her down.

'Micky, wake up,' Emmy cried.

She tried to push him away, but his grip on her arms was too tight. He wasn't in bed with her, he was fighting for his life, and she needed to protect herself. His hands on her arms were so tight she couldn't move, his grip crushing. She was an enemy he needed to defeat to stay alive.

'Micky, wake up.'

His eyes opened, but he did not see her; he was somewhere else; somewhere terrifying.

'Micky.' Emmy sobbed.

'Sailor, come to attention.' Emmy heard the order.

Micky heard the order. He stopped struggling with her, let her free. Emmy scrambled out of the bed as Micky's father took his son's hands.

'Michael Brannigan, come to attention.'

Micky stood to attention. His eyes focused on his father, his legs failed him, and he slid to the floor, his back to the bed. His father sat beside him and took him in his arms.

'Emmy. Where's Emmy?' Micky cried. 'Did I hurt Emmy, Dad? Where's Emmy?'

Emmy wiped the blood from her lip with the back of her hand. 'I'm here, Micky. You didn't hurt me. I'm here.'

She took Micky out of his father's arms and sat on the floor with him. His father took the blanket from the bed, wrapped it around their half-naked bodies and left the room.

A while later, Emmy steadied herself on the kitchen door frame. 'He's asleep,' she said.

'Did you leave the light on?' Kate asked.

'Yes.'

Michael Brannigan helped her sit and Kate poured the tea, the pot clattering on the cup.

'What happened to Micky?' Emmy asked.

'We don't …' Kate replied. She looked into her husband's eyes and said, 'I don't know.' She held her husband's hand.

'We must respect his wishes, Kate.'

'I know,' Kate said.

'Micky has been a prisoner of war in North Vietnam for the past four years, Emmaline,' Michael said.

Emmy sucked in air.

'He came home to us in March this year. His body is beginning to recover, but his mind … will take longer. One day, in the middle of May, he told me he needed to go to Australia. He couldn't tell me why, but I understood. He needed to be where there was a memory of you; where you had been; where you might be one day,' Michael said.

He looked at Kate, a memory in his eyes, understanding in his eyes.

'We are hoping that finding you and Mia might help him find some peace.'

Emmy nodded. She had seen Micky's body and his mind. She wiped her cheeks, realised her face hurt, and the hot tea stung the cut on her lip as she sipped from the cup. She put the cup down, reached around the back of her neck and undid the clasp there.

'This is yours,' she said to Kate.

Michael took the chain and put it around Kate's neck. He rested his forehead on hers as he did this. Emmy knew a love like that could only come from almost losing each other. *Like I almost lost Micky.*

'I have to go,' she said.

'I will call you a taxi,' Michael Brannigan said.

Chapter Seventeen

Emmaline

Emmy sat on the sand and watched her children build sandcastles. Her little brothers, now twelve, and her daughter, not quite four. The sun shone, one of those wonderful, warm winter days, the days she had missed.

Mia had fitted into her extended family like she had always been there. The boys, especially Joey, doted on her and, to Emmy's surprise, her mother had fallen in love with Mia at first sight.

Could she have stayed at home after all? But it was done now, and she would never know.

Jacob called her name and she rose to meet him; they were the only people on the beach, apart from a few surfers catching the waves rolling in. The wind had been blowing gently for ten minutes.

'You were late home, Emmy,' he said. They stood together, looking out at the waves.

'I know.' She didn't want to do this now.

'Emmy, you can't go back to him. You can't let him back into your life after all you've had to do.'

'Don't, Jacob,' Emmy said. 'Don't. You don't know …'

'I don't know what?'

'You don't know anything about me,' Micky said from behind them.

Emmy could see Jacob's anger: he was protecting her as he'd always done. Jacob took her arm and she grimaced. He pushed the sleeve of her jumper up to her elbow and said to Micky. 'I didn't do that.'

Then he called the children.

Micky stared at her arm, his face white.

Emmy pulled her sleeve down, gathered up the towels and plastic toys and put them in her bag; she joined the children as they followed Jacob up the grass embankment. Micky stood alone.

At the top of the embankment, sandy feet dried off, towels and plastic toys tossed into the boot of an old FC Holden, the children piled into the back seat.

'I'll meet you at home,' Emmy said.

The look on Jacob's face startled her. She turned away from him, waved to the children and watched the car drive away.

Micky was sitting on a bench in the middle tier of the embankment. When she joined him, he pushed the sleeves of her jumper up. 'Emmy,' he whispered.

His fingerprints – black, blue, yellow, angry marks – were visible on her arms. She had covered the bruise on her cheek with concealer and face powder, which Emmy didn't think Micky could see, but the cut on her lip was visible. He ran his finger across her lips and wiped the powder from her face.

'Emmy, I'm sorry.'

'You didn't know what you were doing,' she said.

'But I did this.'

Micky

Micky stared at her: he'd done that. Her face: the powder did not hide the bruise on her cheek; no lipstick could hide the cut on her lip. He didn't remember; his nightmare made sure of that.

He did remember being alone for weeks, for months; he remembered darkness, hunger, pain, torture. He remembered going crazy, wishing he was dead. But he had promised Emmy.

He had promised her he would come back for her. He would not let her down. He would do whatever he had to. He would stay alive as long as he could.

There was so much he needed to tell her. There was so much he could never tell her.

'Four years,' he said. 'Some of the guys were there for longer. William got sick ... I don't remember when ... time meant nothing, maybe around September that first year. He was released, *a goodwill gesture.* Our parents knew we were alive then.'

His parents didn't know what was happening to him. He would never tell them; he would never tell anyone.

'My mother tried to find you,' he said.

'I know.'

'Simon died, Emmy.' He forced the words out – they cut, held too much memory.

'Oh, Micky, I'm sorry,' Emmy said. Her hand gripped his, 'I'm sorry.'

'Sometime in the next summer. I miss ... He was injured when we were captured. We had to support him when we were paraded through the streets of Hanoi ... we were the enemy.' He took a breath. Should he tell Emmy anymore? There was so much she could never know.

'Simon wouldn't write letters for them. He wouldn't say they were treating us well. He wouldn't condemn our war effort. It was what they wanted. I was weak.'

'Micky.' Emmy shook her head; she ran her fingers down his chest, down the scar she knew was under his shirt. The scar he knew was under his shirt. She caressed his face, pulled his hands together and held them tight.

'He couldn't walk. He didn't want to go home to Becky like that, but he tried to stay alive. In the end, he couldn't fight anymore. I held him ... I couldn't help him ... he died. He never saw his daughter; never knew she was alive.'

He took a breath, his throat tight. Then he swallowed and said, 'When they found out who his father was … I had to write to the Admiral tell him Simon had been treated well … At least he had a proper funeral, his body went home … I had to … they made …' He couldn't talk anymore, pushed those memories away and remembered Emmy.

He pulled her into his arms; her body fitted into his like it should always be there. He was whole when she was there, but he had hurt her. What might have happened if his father hadn't come home?

The next day at Luige's Café, Emmy ordered pasta to share. She ordered chips for Mia and coffee for herself and him.

Mia sat next to him and asked, 'Who are you?'

She was a cheeky, precocious child, and he fell in love with her. *Emmy's daughter, my daughter.* He did owe Jacob a lot.

'I'm your … I'm Micky.'

She put her little hand out and said, 'How do you do, Micky?'

He smiled; might have laughed. Happiness floated around him; he hadn't felt that for a long time.

'How do you do, Mia?' he said and held her little hand. Emmy smiled across the table at him. Could he have this life?

After lunch, they strolled on the grassed esplanade and Mia ran around on the lawn. When he tired, he sat with Emmy by the sandpit and watched Mia play. Emmy rested her hand on his knee.

'Where have you been, Emmy. What happened to you?'

'It was cold in London, Micky. We were cold.' He pulled her close to keep the wind away.

'I'm not sure I knew what I was thinking. I just needed to go, get away before someone took Mia away from me. That was all I could think of, so I went.'

Emmy folded her hands into his chest. They were cold, and

he took them in his palms and rubbed them.

'Jacob came to London after Christmas. His grandmother had died, and he'd learnt some of the truth about his family; that he has a brother and sister. He found addresses and names of people his grandmother knew in London. Those people gave him an address in Amsterdam. He didn't find his family there, but he found out his real name. We went back to London, then we went to Israel. It took Jacob more than six months, but he found his brother – he lives on a Kibbutz – but he has not found his sister. Mia and I went with him … he helped us …'

Emmy looked at Mia playing in the sand.

'What?' he asked.

Her forehead furrowed as she thought, then she shook her head and continued. 'Jacob wanted to find out about his family. His brother found us a room on the Kibbutz.'

Emmy spoke quietly, her face expressionless. Her hands hadn't warmed up as they should, and he blew on them and rubbed them a little harder.

She stopped talking and watched their child playing.

'Emmy?' he asked.

'Nothing,' Emmy said.

'Tell me.'

Emmy turned to face him. 'There is a children's house at the Kibbutz, part of the communal thing, sharing everything. All the children live there. Mia had to live there. I don't want …'

'We can …,' he said.

How could he offer Emmy anything, knowing what he'd done? What he *could* do?

'Stay here.'

'Maybe.' Emmy stopped talking. She turned her head away from him and took a deep breath before saying. 'It's a different way of living. Not bad. Everything you need, you work for; everything you make, you share. I've done some teaching, which was wonderful. We work in the fields, the kitchens, we do military training, that's difficult. I don't think I could pull a trigger, but I'm told I would if I had to …' Emmy hesitated.

He looked into her eyes: she was holding something back, not wanting him to see, but he could.

'Sometimes Mia spends the night with us, but only because Jacob, *my husband*, is a welder, and his skills are needed. Some of the younger mothers support me, but the older people don't – there is always a hierarchy. It interferes with my contribution to the group if I want to bring up my child, I'm told.'

'Emmy.'

'Mia's our daughter, Micky. I'm scared that one day she will be taken away and never come back. I know that won't happen, I know I'm being silly, but …'

He kissed the fingers he was holding.

Mia was his daughter, but she called Jacob, Papa. Emmy called Jacob, *husband*.

The bruises on Emmy's face showed through the makeup she had used.

That was his fault.

Chapter Eighteen

Emmaline

There was a knock on the door.

'Emmy there's an old man to see you,' Emmy's brother called.

'Don't be rude, Jimmy,' Emmy said as she came to the door. 'Oh.'

'Can I talk to you?' Michael Brannigan said. A taxi was at the end of the pathway, waiting.

'Mama, can you mind, Mia?' Emmy called.

'Where is she?'

'In the front room with Joey.'

The taxi ride to the Ocean Beach Hotel seemed to take forever. The walk up the stairs to the lounge was longer. Emmy could hardly stand by the time Michael Brannigan sat her in a chair near the window. He ordered whisky for himself and coffee for her at the bar, then sat on the chair opposite her.

'Micky's gone,' he said.

'Gone?' she heard herself say, like someone else was talking.

The waiter bought the drinks. Michael swirled his, and Emmy picked her coffee up. The contents trickled down the side of the cup; she put the cup to her lips.

Rain battered the windows, and the ocean across the road roared. The sandy shore washed away, and she couldn't tell where the grey sky ended and the grey ocean began.

'Gone where?'

'He hasn't told us. He has asked me not to try and find out, to trust he knows what he's doing. Kate is distraught.'

'Why?'

He reached across the coffee table and placed his fingers on her cheek. He knew what was under the makeup.

'It wasn't his fault,' Emmy said.

'No, but he understands what it means to both of you. I can't tell you what happened to Micky. I know some of the details and I can guess the rest. I will keep that from Kate. There are some things a mother shouldn't know.'

Emmy looked out the window. The winter weather pounded the building, shaking the glass. If she could, she would run; run as far as she could until she outran the pain. But there was nowhere to go; she could never outrun Micky.

'He asked me to give you this.'

Michael Brannigan handed her an envelope. 'Would you like me to leave you alone while you read it?'

She shook her head.

My darling, Micky had written.

> *Please forgive me.*
>
> *The life I want with you would be no good for you. It is too dangerous for you to be with me.*
>
> *You are safer with Jacob, he cares for you and has looked after you and Mia all these years.*
>
> *I cannot forgive what I did to you. I will always love you, but you must be safe, and being away from me is the only way.*
>
> *My father has promised not to interfere in my decisions, and I trust him to do that. I ask you to keep in touch with my parents, for their sake.*
>
> *Look after Mia for me. What a lovely little girl she is. I love her and I hope one day you will tell her who I am. I hope she will understand how much I love her.*
>
> *Forgive me.*

Emmy stared at the words on the paper. Why couldn't she cry? That would have felt better because, right now, she felt nothing.

Michael took her hand and said, 'Emmaline, I can only tell you this … knowing Kate was waiting for me kept me alive. And I know for Micky having you waiting for him kept him alive.'

'Where will he go?' she asked.

'He has told me one of the POWs, a senior officer, has set up a support group for those who want it, somewhere in Mexico. I am hoping he will go there no matter how long it takes him. I have promised him I won't track him down; he knows I can do this, but I will keep my word to him.'

He was telling her not to ask him; not to put him in that position. She would not.

'Emmaline, I need to ask you one more thing.'

She could see he wasn't sure what she would say, but she could see how important the question was.

'Will you let Kate meet Mia?'

Her granddaughter, there could only be one answer.

'I would like that.' Emmy said.

On Sunday, Emmy sat on the swing in the backyard of a little home on Bellevue Terrace in Fremantle. The storm of the previous day had blown itself out and a winter sun now warmed the day. Her daughter sat on the back veranda and drew pictures with her grandmother.

The anguish of yesterday hovered around her. She had to let Micky go; had to let him make that decision. She did not want to.

Michael Brannigan bought coffee in mugs out the back door; he placed one on the table for Kate then he sat on the bottom step overlooking the garden. Emmy joined him, and he gave her the other cup of coffee.

'Thank you for this,' he said.

'Mr Brannigan …'

'Michael,' he said.

'Michael,' Emmy said. 'You don't have to thank me. It is wonderful for Mia to meet her grandmother. To meet both of you.'

She had told Mia they were going to visit her grandparents. Emmy had decided there had been too much deception, too many lies. She couldn't tell her who Micky was – not yet – but she could know his parents. Mia was surprised – she already had grandparents, Oma and Opa.

Emmy told her, 'You are a very lucky girl you have two lots of grandparents like many children in this country. You will call them Grandma and Grandpa. They are excited to be meeting you.'

'What will you do, Emmaline?' Michael Brannigan asked.

I'm going to Mexico, and I will bring Micky home. We will make a life together; he will be Mia's father, and I will help him get better. That's what she wanted to do, wanted to say. But she said, 'We are booked to go back to Israel next week.'

'As you have no doubt worked out, Kate and I are the benefactors Frank Kelly told you about.'

Emmy nodded; she had worked that out. How lucky she had been. What would have happened to Mia without them?

'So you will not take offence if I tell you our family is comfortable. Kate bought this house when her father died. It is the home she grew up in, and it gives us a home when we visit. This house will be empty if you would like to use it.'

She could do that.

'I retired from the Navy a few years back, but you never leave. My mother and I owned a successful business in Portland; that business is now mine. My daughters run the business. We have a home on the West Coast not far from San Francisco,' Michael said.

Somewhere else Emmy always wanted to go … but London hadn't been what she thought it would, had it. She was older and wiser now.

'You are always welcome there,' Michael said. Then he said, 'I almost lost Kate and Micky when he was born. I was injured, I thought she would be better off without me.'

Mia came clomping down the stairs. 'Mama, can you push me on the swing … *please.*'

Emmy went to stand, and Michael said, 'May I push you?'

Mia studied him. 'Yes, Grandpa,' she said.

He pushed himself up from the step and took her hand. For the first time, Emmy noticed he walked with a limp. Then he straightened his back and corrected his gait as he strode to the swing.

Kate sat on the step beside her. 'She looks too much like Micky,' she said.

'Yes.'

'I don't know how we survived when we got the news Micky was missing. We clung to hope. William told us he was alive when he came home. When Micky's letters reached Joe, the Admiral, and Simon's Becky, we knew he was still alive, but we never heard from him in all those years, never knew what was happening to him.'

Kate looked out over the garden at Michael pushing Mia on the swing. Emmy reached out and held her hand.

'I hoped and prayed you would keep Micky's child,' Kate said.

Mia was laughing and calling out for her grandfather to push her higher.

Kate wiped her cheeks and said, 'They always think they have to protect us. He thought I would be better off without him; his injuries were so bad. He was wrong.'

'That's what Micky's doing,' Emmy said.

'Yes. That's what he's doing. They don't understand we can look after ourselves and we will look after them. But Micky is right at the moment. He blames himself for so much. If he hurt you again, he would not recover.'

Emmy caught her breath.

She would go back to Israel with Jacob and keep Micky safe. That was something she could do.

Micky

Micky stared out the window as the plane flew over the top of thick white clouds. He needed to go, to get away before he changed his mind. Emmy would try and stop him if he gave her a chance. He did not. He was on a flight to Sydney, with an overnight stop and then to New Zealand on his way to Hawaii.

After his release from prison, he'd visited Simon's parents. They no longer lived in Hawaii where Simon had grown up. The Admiral had hugged him, shaken his hand and looked him in the eyes, letting him know he knew he'd done all he could for his son. That he was allowed to be alive … it was not his fault Simon had died. It was more than Micky could do for himself.

Simon's mother had held Micky tight and wiped his tears away like she'd done when he was a little boy, but her grief over Simon's death overpowered him. He could see as much as she loved him and was happy to see him, he wasn't her boy. Her boy wasn't coming home.

Now he would visit Becky; he could do that for Simon. He had written to Becky after Simon died, after he'd written to his father. But he was only allowed to say he had died, that he'd become ill and even though he'd received the best medical care, he did not survive. All lies. He hadn't known if she'd received his letter until March that year.

He would tell her what he could, if she wanted to know, there was too much she couldn't know. He had promised Simon he wouldn't let him go home to Becky broken and a burden to her. That promise he'd kept: he didn't want to keep it; he wanted Simon to live, but he couldn't stop him from dying. He would not ask Becky's forgiveness; he could not ask anyone's forgiveness.

He closed his eyes but couldn't sleep. Instead, he thought of Emmy and Mia. He had a photograph. Emmy carried a Polaroid camera in her bag, and he'd taken a snap of them together in the park the other day. He would hold on to that. Emmy had to be safe, and her being away from him was the only way to ensure it.

Chapter Nineteen

Emmaline

Emmy sat with her father on the step watching the children play on the back lawn. Her childhood had ended when the twins were born; her father needed her help to keep the family together, yet she would not have changed a thing.

'I'm glad you came home,' he said.

'Me too.'

'She's a lovely little girl.' They both looked at Mia sitting on the grass with her uncles.

'The boys missed you,' he said.

'Oh Papa, I've missed them too. How big they are now.' They had grown up since she'd last seen them, still little boys, but not for long. 'I should have come home sooner. I'm sorry.'

'No, Emmy. You have to live your life, and I'm glad you did. Look at my little granddaughter; you gave us her.'

'Mama!'

'She was okay. She missed you; I told her you had gone to Melbourne on holiday. When you didn't come home for the school holidays, I told her you would be back for Christmas. The postcard from London surprised us, but when Jacob went to London after his grandmother died, I knew he would look after you.'

'I'm sorry, Papa.'

'Don't say that,' John Cannon said. 'You were right. Mama wasn't ready to hear about a baby. I didn't tell her you were pregnant; that you would have the baby adopted. I told her you were on holiday. She liked getting the picture postcards. Israel was a surprise. I trusted you would be okay in the Kibbutz. It was good Jacob found his brother.'

'Micky's parents visited me in June after you left for Melbourne,' he said. 'I told them you had gone there and that Father Kelly had arranged a place for you. You never told me where, Emmy. I wasn't sure what you would have wanted. They had been told Micky was missing, presumed dead. His father told me they had received the letter you wrote to Micky telling him you were pregnant. Micky's mother was desperate. I hoped you wouldn't mind; I couldn't tell them much more.'

Missing, presumed dead. Emmy's heart skipped a beat. *Presumed dead.* She hadn't known. What would she have done if she'd known?

John Cannon reached out and touched the bruise hidden on Emmy's cheek. Emmy took a breath and said, 'Micky's gone away … to keep me safe.' Her father put his arm around her; she was *his little girl*, and Emmy let herself be that little girl, just for a moment. Then she wiped her tears and murmured, 'To keep me safe.'

Emmy told her father what he needed to know about her injured face.

'Stay home with us, Emmy. Mama loves Mia. We can help you look after her. Mama wasn't surprised when I told her about Mia; when I told her you were bringing a child home. She knew Micky was Mia's father; I didn't have to tell her,' John Cannon said. 'I have tried to protect her; she has suffered so much, but I should have let her make more of these decisions.'

'She is stronger than we think, Papa, to survive all she has, but I had to do what I did. She was so sick after the twins were born.'

Emmy looked at her father. His brown hair was now grey; he had worked hard these last twenty years, and it showed. He was still fit and healthy, though, but his shoulders slouched a little more than they should, and he still had two boys to guide to adulthood.

'You can have a room here. Your brother doesn't need it anymore,' he said.

Hank had moved into shared accommodation with two friends. His birthdate had not been selected by the national service lottery, so Mama hadn't had to suffer that. He still came home for meals on the weekends and to do his washing.

It would be easy to stay home with her Mama and Papa. Go to work, with Mia looked after. Mia sleeping in a bed near her, and not living in a children's house.

But Emmy wouldn't. It had always been a two-way trip to see her family, for Mia to meet her family.

Mia called Jacob 'Papa'; Emmy couldn't abandon him; he had been there for her when she needed him the most.

She hadn't expected to stay home; hadn't expected to see Micky; hadn't expected so much heartache.

Chapter Twenty

Micky

Micky looked in the mirror, the face looking back unshaved, the hair dirty and unkempt, he didn't like that person. He splashed water on his face. He'd been drinking – it helped him sleep. If you drank until you passed out, you had a few hours of peace, but you had to wake up, then it started over again. He didn't want to be that man.

He'd been in Hawaii for two weeks. When he wasn't sleeping on the beach in a drunken stupor, he sat on Becky's veranda and watched the waves roll over Waikiki beach. That would be a place to make it all go away. He could swim out there and never come back, but he couldn't do that to Emmy and Mia. He might never see them again, but he couldn't do that. He loved them too much. He splashed more water on his face, needing to tidy himself up.

He filled the sink with hot water, lathered his face and pulled the blade through the stubble, his unsteady hand finally finishing the task. He turned on the shower and waited for the room to fill with steam before he took his shirt off. If he didn't look, he couldn't see his scars in the mist, but they were there.

Becky kept his clothes clean for him, and she never pressured him for more information than he was willing to tell. He hadn't intended to stay, but she had asked him, telling him William was due in for two weeks' leave. So he'd stayed.

Simon's little girl, Amelia, was as much like Simon as Mia was like him. She had his blond hair and blue eyes; it was hard seeing her knowing Simon had never met her. He was thankful he had met Mia; was grateful Emmy knew he loved her and hadn't abandoned her.

Leaving Emmy was the hardest thing he'd ever done. He could never see her again, never put her through that pain, never put himself through that pain. Constant pain, eating him. Maybe it would lessen if he didn't see her again. He wanted a life with Emmy and Mia, but it was too far away. He had hurt her – how much worse it might have been. He couldn't think about that; he had to be strong. He dried off, combed his hair and looked at the bloodshot eyes in the mirror. That man wasn't who Emmy needed; she was safe with Jacob.

On a warm summer day, the air filled with frangipani and hibiscus scent, Micky and Becky sat on the veranda. Becky had filled glasses with cordial and had placed wine and beer in a cooler. On the table were plates of cheese, fruit, dips and crackers. Amelia played on the grass at the front of the house.

They heard William coming along the street, his radio blaring and him singing. Amelia stopped playing, looked at her mother and yelled, 'William's home.'

'Yes,' Becky said. 'Go on, go meet him.'

The little girl ran out the gate and bounded down the road; William picked her up and tossed her in the air. She screamed as he pretended to drop her; wrapped her arms tight around his neck as he carried her through the gate. He strode across the lawn and stopped at the veranda step. Putting Amelia on the ground, he looked into Micky's eyes.

There was no need for explanation; Micky could see what was going on. Becky stood and hesitated, then she kissed William on the cheek. He accepted the kiss and showed no surprise.

Micky stood back from William. He had missed him, the friendship of years tested. He hadn't expected this though. Should he have? – the common bond over a lost love, a friendship that grew into more.

William was not expected to survive when he left Vietnam; Micky hadn't known until his own release that he had. He stepped forward and offered his hand to William.

William accepted his hand, then pulled him into his arms and hugged him like he would never let him go. It felt good in his arms; he was strong, healthy and happy.

'Stop it, stop it,' Becky cried. 'Stop it!'

Micky was rolling around on the lawn with William. It wasn't a fair fight, William trying not to hurt him, but Micky let his anger and frustration overtake him – laughable if it hadn't been them fighting. He still had no strength, could barely walk unaided, and still struggled to breathe at any exertion.

He had come home from swimming and found Becky and William in each other's arms. Becky was Simon's wife, Amelia was Simon's daughter. Emmy should have been his wife, Mia was his daughter.

'Stop it, Micky! What would Simon say?' Becky cried again.

Micky heard Becky. What was he doing? Why was he fighting William? He lowered his fists and slumped on the lawn. William grabbed his wrists and sat opposite him.

'Micky, come on,' William said. 'We didn't plan this. It just happened. It would never have happened if Simon was alive.'

Micky looked him in the eyes. 'I know,' he said.

He lowered his eyes and turned his head away, not wanting William to see his tears. William held him until he stopped shaking, then he helped him to his feet, and they sat together on the veranda.

'I'm sorry,' Micky said. 'I'll be leaving tomorrow.'

'You don't have to do that.'

'Yes, I do.'

He needed to leave; he needed to sort himself out. There had to be a place where the hurt wasn't so strong, where he could find some peace.

'How long did it take you?' he asked.

William hesitated then said, 'I wasn't there as long as you, but I remember … the pain … the fear. Somewhere, sometime, it became less of who I was, less of what I only thought about. Having Becky and Amelia has helped, but then there was the added guilt about Simon, but we came to understand he would have wanted us to be happy.'

Micky nodded.

'What happened to Emmaline?' William asked.

Micky sucked in his breath. *Emmaline.* Even the name hurt.

'I'm no good for her,' was all he could say.

Chapter Twenty-one

September 1973

Emmaline

Emmy lay flat in the dust. It was her twenty-fifth birthday, almost Mia's fourth birthday. She never thought she would spend it like this. Projectiles flew overhead, and she shuddered. Only training. It felt too real. She was dirty, smelly and hot. The drill, as they called it, had been going on all day.

She'd had enough of the yelling. Enough of being dirty and, like a petulant child, she wanted to go home, not back to the Kibbutz, but home, away from a place where she had to fight to keep Mia with her; where she cried in her bed when she could not. Away from the fear of not knowing if Mia was safe, not having her tucked in a bed close by. She wanted a place to call home.

Emmy hadn't known how the truth would be taken when they moved into the Kibbutz in 1971; it was easier to lie. Jacob and Emmy were married: that was the story. Mia was their child. There were many silly questions because Mia looked nothing like either of them.

Jacob's grandmother had kept most of the family history a secret from him; she had bought him up as a Christian and given him her name. His brother, Karl Becker, had become a friend and mentor to Jacob, teaching him what he remembered of their family and encouraging him to learn about the Jewish faith.

Emmy wanted the deception to end, so they told Karl the truth when they returned from Australia or what he needed to know about the truth. He accepted they had lied to him and believed they had told him the truth.

He also said, 'Emmy will have to leave. You can stay, Jacob, and so can Mia – she has done no wrong.'

Jacob would not do that, and they were making plans to travel to Berlin, where he knew his family had lived before the war, where he hoped to find some trace of his sister.

Karl said, 'I have not been able to find our sister. All I have is her name, Inge Becker. She could have changed it.'

Jacob wanted to try. Michael Brannigan had given him names and contact numbers in West Berlin and told him to use them. Michael had also insisted on giving Emmy money for future fares and expenses. She'd hidden that in a bank account in Mia's name.

Emmy and Jacob had been looking after each other most of their lives: she would help him with his search, and she hoped someone was helping Micky with his.

'Papa's home,' Mia called.

'Papa Jacob,' Emmy corrected.

She'd been home from the training camp for a few hours, had washed the dirt and sweat off her body and out of her hair, and she'd put on clean clothes and brushed and tied Mia's hair up. There was time together in the afternoon in their room before the communal living started in the kitchen and dining room, and the fight to keep Mia at night began.

They still passed themselves off as Mia's parents. Emmy was tired of the lies and the fighting and would be happy to travel to Berlin, where she was going to be Mia's mother, and Jacob would be her friend.

She had started by teaching Mia to call Jacob by his name. Even though she was young, Emmy wanted her to know who

Jacob really was. One day she would know her father.

'Papa Jacob!' Mia cried as she ran into his arms. He spun her around and held her tight before putting her on the floor. He kissed Emmy on the cheek.

She looked into his face. 'What?' she said.

He'd been away for the past three weeks at a training camp, and he'd spent time in Tele Viv arranging fares and selling the last of his grandmother's jewellery. His eyes sparkled.

She knew that look. 'Jacob?' she queried.

'I've met someone.'

'Jacob,' Emmy squealed.

'I hope you won't mind.'

'What's her name? When do I get to meet her?'

'Peta,' he said. He looked at the floor.

'Peta … that's pretty,' Emmy said.

Jacob scuffed his toe on the floor.

'What is it, Jacob?'

He cleared his throat and said, 'His name is Peter.' He was looking at her.

'Oh!' Emmy said.

She looked into his eyes: he was happy; he was in love. Why hadn't she seen this before? What had she been doing? His reluctance to meet other girls, his apparent obsession with her. She was safe: he knew how she loved him; knew that was all she could give him. She had never lied to him, never told him otherwise. It was safe for him to love her.

The times they had spent in bed, a quiet acceptance of each other's physical needs, a gentle use of each other. She couldn't give him any more, and he hadn't asked for any more. She loved him so much.

'When do I meet him?' she said and threw her arms around him.

Jacob spun her around like she was Mia, then they sat on the floor, Mia between them.

'You don't mind?' he said.

'How could I mind.' She caressed his cheek.

His anger and his frustration … how hard it must have been for him growing up, not knowing who he was, not being able to know who he was. All the silly jokes, the name-calling, the boys so cruel without knowing what they were saying. Times were changing a bit too slowly.

'How did you meet?' Emmy asked.

'We met in the supermarket. My basket was on the floor. He put some of his shopping into it … a classic tactic, apparently.' He took a deep breath and said, 'We've only known each other for two weeks, but I'm … I'm sorry, Emmy … I understand about you and Micky now. I couldn't forgive him for what he did to you. I never understood how you loved him or how he loved you.'

Emmy swallowed thickly. It still hurt to talk about Micky.

'Oh, Jacob.' She rested her head on his shoulder, and he wrapped her and Mia in his arms.

Peter came into Emmy's life two weeks later. He was a little older than her and Jacob; he knew who he was and when and where he could be that person.

He was on holiday, visiting the Christian sites in Israel. He took Emmy and Jacob out to see these, surprised they hadn't already done so. It also surprised Emmy that they hadn't done this but working on the Kibbutz seemed to take all the time.

Mia had taken to him. He had dark hair and olive skin; he wasn't as tall as Jacob, and was more solid and stronger. There was a familiarity about him Emmy couldn't place, like she should or could have known him. Perhaps his accent, he sounded like Micky.

Did Mia see that too?

Chapter Twenty-two

Emmaline

On the celebrated Jewish holy day of Yom Kippur, Emmy was excused from prayers, a Christian girl living on a Kibbutz did not need to attend. Almost the truth.

Instead, Emmy picked oranges in the orchard, her face warm; she'd rolled up her sleeves to catch the last of the summer sun on her skin, knowing the weather would soon turn cold. The Kibbutz sat in a valley of rolling hills, the land covered in green grass and trees, but some places were barren and covered in gravel which reminded her of home.

She heard the screech of engines and, shading her eyes, looked in the direction of the sound. There was more than one plane in the pale blue sky. Which was odd. The planes flew low over her, then she heard the explosions. Looking down the hill to where the buildings stood, she saw smoke. And ran.

At the top of the road leading into the settlement, she fell to her knees, wailing. The settlement was burning. People were running, trying to put out the fires. The children's house! Mia was in the children's house! Gone, just a pile of rubble, smoke and flames.

'Emmy!' Jacob called to her.

She looked up into his blood-stained face. She couldn't move … if she moved …

'Mia!' she heard herself say above all the noise. 'Mia!'

'The children are safe.'

'Mia!'

'She's safe … all the children are safe,' he repeated and held out his hand. 'Come on. You can't stay here.'

Emmy tried to move, but her legs wouldn't support her. Jacob pulled her up, and she leaned on him until her legs began to obey her thoughts. They ran down the road together. She could hear the screech of engines getting closer.

The world slowed around her. The road in front of her disappeared. She couldn't hear anything. Emmy looked at Jacob; he was holding her hand, trying to let his grip loose as he fell to the ground. She felt the ground slam into her. Then she felt nothing.

Emmy's eyelids flickered. Light, noise, there was so much noise: people, machines beeping, someone's heartbeat, her heartbeat.

'Mia!' She tried to move, but a hand restrained her.

A voice said, 'She's awake, sir.'

'Don't try and get up,' she was told.

'Mia!' She tried to push the hand away. How long had she been here? 'Mia!'

'She's safe.' Another voice, a voice she remembered.

Emmy blinked her eyes open. She lay on a cot, the type seen in war movies. She was not alone in the building. Was it a building; it was full of people on cots? Medical staff hurried about. People in uniform hurried about. A machine beeped – her heartbeat. When she moved, the beeping sped up.

Her chest felt on fire. Her head pounded. Emmy looked into the face of the speaker. 'William?'

William held her hand and said, 'Mia is safe.'

'Jacob. Where's Jacob?'

'I'm here, Emmy.' He stood next to her cot, his arm in a sling, cuts and bruises on his face.

Emmy closed her eyes. *Micky.*

She heard Jacob call her name, but she could not open her eyes.

Emmy was dreaming: Cottesloe beach on a summer evening, Micky and his friends body surfing. She didn't want it to end.

Emmy opened her eyes. Jacob was sitting by the cot.

'What happened?' she asked through dry lips. 'Water?' she asked.

Jacob held her head up and put a glass of water to her lips. She took a sip. 'What ...?' It was too hard to move.

A doctor came to the bed. *No, not a doctor, a medic.*

'You have a bad concussion and some cracked ribs,' William said.

'Micky?' Emmy asked.

William shook his head, and Emmy wiped tears and hope away. She sucked in pain as William helped her sit. 'Mia?'

'She okay, Emmy. She's on board with Peter,' Jacob said.

'Onboard?'

'The USNC Jackson,' William said. 'She's tied up in Port. We have taken some of our citizens on board for safety.'

'What day is it?'

'You've been asleep on and off for three days,' William told her.

'You can bring Mia in if you like,' he told Jacob.

Jacob kissed her forehead and said, 'I'll see you soon.' Emmy grabbed his hand and said, 'Thank you.'

He smiled at her. 'Always,' he said.

William went about his duties, checking her pulse, listening to her chest, looking in her eyes, then he sat on the chair by the cot. She wanted to ask him so much.

'The last time I saw Micky was in Hawaii, back in July,' William said before she could ask. 'He was getting better physically, but he still had a lot of shit to sort out.'

'I know,' Emmy said. She was so tired of being strong.

'I don't know where he went after that. He hasn't been in touch since then.'

'Do you think he will?'

William shrugged.

Emmy closed and opened her eyes, blinking the tears away.

'Where are we?' she asked

'In a field hospital. Our ship was in port when the war began, and we've been able to help with the wounded.'

'What war?'

What war? When did this happen? There had been training, but she never thought anything would come of it.

'Syria and Egypt attacked Israel on October 6,' William said. 'Rest now. Mia will be here soon.'

Emmy reached for his hand, and he gave it to her.

'Are you well, William?' Emmy asked.

'I am, Emmaline. I have found a place to call home, to find peace. I hope you and Micky will be able to do that too.'

She closed her eyes.

'Mama,' Emmy heard. 'Mama.'

'I'm okay, Mia.' She tried to sit but couldn't, so Jacob helped her up and sat Mia on the bed beside her. She wrapped her arms around her daughter and whispered gentle words in her ear. Caressing her face, she checked to make sure Mia had no injuries. She would never show Mia the pain she was in.

Emmy left the hospital three days later, her ribs bandaged, her head throbbing. The war was raging, but the Syrians had withdrawn back across the strip, away from the Kibbutz. The building they lived in had been damaged but not destroyed. Emmy gathered all she could, most importantly her passports, banking details and the tickets for the flight. Jacob's brother wished them well and she thought he meant it.

The plane flew out of Tele Viv at 6.00 pm on October 12th, 1973. It was warm and sunny when they left Israel, cold and gloomy when they arrived in Germany.

Berlin in October was indeed cold, and the days were shorter. Emmy wore her coat often. Jacob searched East and West Berlin for any information about this sister, but even with all the help Michael Brannigan had given him, he couldn't find any trace of her.

Emmy knew her mother had lived in Berlin and found her family with ease. She knew the family name – she had seen it on the back of a photograph she'd found in her mother's top drawer when she was helping with the twins. In the picture were five children dressed in uniforms. Emmy thought, *maybe Brownies or Scouts*. On the back, written in German, it said, Die Hartmann-Kinder. Emmy wrote this name in her book of secrets, then she put the photo back in Mama's drawer.

Emmy learnt that her grandmother had died several years before, and her mother's sisters shared the home, a flat in a five-storey workers' accommodation building on the east side of the Berlin Wall.

The indifference they showed to her and Mia was a shock. They had been polite and shared coffee and small talk, which Jacob helped her understand. Emmy could see they were confused and didn't know how to react to her; she didn't stay long.

The younger of her mother's sisters showed her to the door, hugged her and said, 'Ich bin glücklich Gerta hat ein besseres Leben. Auf Wiedersehen, Emmaline.'

Jacob translated for her: 'I'm happy Gerta made a better life. Goodbye, Emmaline.'

There was no need to stay in Berlin. Peter was waiting for Jacob in London. Emmy realised it was more a matter of place than time. When Peter met them on their arrival at Heathrow, he hugged her and tossed Mia in the air, but he only offered Jacob his hand. Emmy could see their desperation to hold each other, but the arrival lounge at Heathrow Airport wasn't the right place. When the taxi pulled up in front of a row of terraced houses in Soho, Peter jumped out and pulled Jacob into his arms, holding him tight. There was no kiss; that had to wait until they were inside, behind closed doors.

Peter was like a brother to her, and if she was honest, he looked a little like her brother Hank, but older and more sophisticated. He insisted Emmy and Mia stay and share Christmas with him and Jacob.

The Christmas they shared was different to the first Christmas Emmy had in London. Peter kept the apartment warm, and there was no shortage of food. Jacob and Peter decorated a tree and made a great fuss of Mia; she was now just over four years old.

Peter refused to take any money from Emmy; she did what she could, buying food and helping with the chores. Jacob, however, struggled when they arrived. She heard him and Peter one night.

'I can't be a kept man,' Jacob had said.

'Don't be silly,' was the reply.

'Don't make fun of me. I've always worked, always paid my own way.' Then there was silence.

'Not fair.' Jacob's voice trembled.

'Shh, you will wake Emmy …'

I am awake.

Soon after, Jacob received an offer of employment. He had been a boilermaker and welder at the car factory in Cottesloe; now he worked in London as a welder, but of jewellery. She had never seen him so happy and content with himself.

Emmy kept in touch with Kate and Michael, sending pictures

and letters of Mia's life. She never asked about Micky or his whereabouts, and they never offered any details. She hadn't planned on staying in London, but Kate and Michael asked her to spend some time with them on a visit they were making in February, so she stayed.

The three-day week, set in place because of a coal miners' strike, ended in March. The weather warmed up. The grass turned green. And trees began to bloom. Emmy was able to get work at the coffee shop on Old Brompton Road, the lack of a working permit dismissed. Mia was enrolled in school, and life settled into a pattern, a pattern terrorism and bag searches disrupted in June and July.

Emmy would not be staying in London for another winter.

Chapter Twenty-three

July 1974

Micky

Micky sat on the bench on the front porch. Daylight would show the green lawn running all the way down to the sandy cove and the harbour. He had stopped struggling for air but was still shaking. Nightmares.

Two in the morning. A warm summer's night. He looked at the sky, where stars peeped out from behind clouds. The moon was still hidden, and the sea was a bowl of black with one or two pinpoints of light. On the few boats in the harbour, some lights were on. He focused on those, on the stars he could see, on the light — *there was no light when the pit door shut.*

His mother pulled her robe together as she sat on the seat beside him. He hadn't meant to wake the household. She took his hand, and he turned his head to look at her. But the light coming out of the hallway was too bright, and he turned back to the black sea.

'Sorry,' he said. 'I didn't want to wake you.'

'I know,' his mother said.

Some days, the memories were far enough away he could live his life, but some days the memories surrounded him, pushed him back into the darkness. He'd spent enough time in Mexico; thought he was ready, wanted to be ready, wanted to be useful. Wanted a life.

He had a family. Emmy had sent pictures of Mia to his

parents, and he knew where she was and what she was doing. It was a family Micky could not have. He couldn't trust himself: he had to keep Emmy safe.

'Write to Emmaline, Micky,' his mother said. 'Let her know where you are, what you are doing.'

'Tell her what, Mum, that I'm still crazy, that I'm always going to be crazy.'

'Don't!' his mother said.

'I should tell her to move on with her life. Find someone else.'

'Do you think she could do that?'

Micky saw a memory on his mother's face.

'I thought I'd lost your father,' she said. Then she said, 'We'd received the letter from Major Smith, missing in action … when Emmy's letter arrived, it gave us hope. Don't leave her without any word from you.'

'Emmy would be better off if I was dead,' Micky said.

'No,' his mother whispered.

'That is enough.' His father's voice behind him wasn't loud, but he jumped to attention.

Micky stared out to sea, out into the blackness as his father helped his mother from the seat. Out the corner of his eye, he saw him wipe the tears from her cheeks and hold her tight before placing his lips on her forehead. He heard him say: 'I'll be up soon.'

The light in the hallway went off, and darkness wrapped around him. He focused on the stars he could see.

His father sat on the bench and said, 'Sit down, Micky. I'm your father, not your commanding officer.'

He could feel the tension his father was controlling as he sat next to him.

'Your mother knows more than you or me what Emmaline is going through,' he said.

The words came out like he was debating whether to tell him.

Then he said, 'I didn't know she was pregnant. I didn't know about you. I thought she would be better off without me. I was cruel and selfish.'

'Selfish?' Micky asked.

'Yes, selfish. I didn't know that until I thought I'd lost her … until I thought I was going to have to live without her.'

'What happened, Dad?' Micky asked.

No one had ever talked about it. He knew his parents weren't married when he was born. He knew his father had suffered injuries.

The moon came out from behind a cloud, and he saw his father's face. Thirty years ago and still etched there.

'It was a long time ago, but sometimes it seems like yesterday, and it will be like that for you one day.'

Micky shook his head. He hoped there might be a time when his life would be different, but the nightmares returned so easy. Could he ever sleep without them?

'The crew was safe,' his father said, 'but I lost the boat. Admiral Daniels – he wasn't an Admiral then – wrote to your mother, told her the boat was lost and I was missing, presumed dead. Being engaged in those days didn't mean your mother had any official status, but Joe knew.'

He stopped talking and looked out into the blackness. Then he said, 'The 'Chief' and my XO came back for me. The Japanese didn't adhere to the *rules of war* regarding prisoners. The war ended before they killed us.'

'Dad.' Micky said.

His father's face was stone, but the cracks were visible in the moonlight. He shook his head and focused on Micky.

'Like you, I thought your mother would be better off without me. For a time, I didn't know if I would walk again. I didn't want to burden her. She almost died when you were born. I almost lost both of you.'

His voice faded away and he stopped talking. Then he placed his hand on Micky's shoulder. 'I could have lost both of you.'

Michael Brannigan pushed himself up off the bench and left his son looking out into the blackness.

Chapter Twenty-four

Micky

Friday, towards the end of July 1974, Micky stood next to a wheelchair. Roy Wallace, his client – not patient, but client – simmered, his hostility boiling.

Micky and Roy, on a hot summer's day, stood in San Francisco overlooking the Golden Gate Bridge, on an outing away from the hostel where Roy lived. Boats sailed on the water, and the old prison spread across the island in the middle of the bay.

Roy had been Micky's client for the past three weeks. Micky didn't wear a uniform but dressed in blue jeans and a white t-shirt with a LA Lakers logo on the front. He wore his black shoes clean and polished.

Roy was angry most days. Micky had learnt being angry was better than being nothing: at least it proved you were alive.

Roy was a regular soldier, injured in Vietnam by a bomb blast early in April 1972. He wouldn't go home to his wife and child, to a town full of pity and stares, to a community who, when they found out the truth about his injuries, didn't know how to treat him – a community that had never lost a war before and wanted someone to blame. The soldiers who fought and died or those who sent them to fight and die?

The hostel was safe. He shared it with others who had experienced what he had; these things were in the notes Micky read.

Micky and Roy went out two or three times a week. Today,

Roy's family joined them. Today, Roy raged and took it out on Micky.

'I guess you spent the war dodging the draft in Canada,' Roy said.

'I spent the war in a prison in Hanoi,' Micky said. It was out before he had time to think, to hold it back.

Roy went pale, and Micky's hands began to tremble.

'Shit, man, what the fuck are you doing here?'

'I …'

When the war ended, the POW's welcome home was jubilant. President Nixon gave a homecoming dinner at the White House. A silver-plated invitation had arrived in the mail, but Micky couldn't attend. Simon was dead. William was back on board the Jackson and, for soldiers like Roy, there was no invitation. For soldiers like Roy, there was no coming home parade: they were not heroes. They were told not to wear their uniform, not to talk about the war. The country was angry and embarrassed.

The relief and love his family had shown on his return were enough. Micky didn't want or need anything else. Simon's death would forever overshadow his homecoming, his friend who had grown up as much in Micky's home as in his own. Micky's family shared the grief over Simon's death with his family; they could not share their joy at Micky's safe return with Simon's family.

Simon's death had to mean something.

'I want to help,' Micky said.

'Who's helping you?' Roy asked.

'I'm …'

Micky couldn't stop the tremble in his hands. His heart was trying to get out of his chest, and he began to sweat. He wanted to do this. It shouldn't be so hard. He thought he was ready. He understood it wasn't his fault he hadn't died, that he had survived, and Simon hadn't. He understood he needed to forgive himself. His body was filling out, he was stronger; the scars in the mirror, he didn't look at too closely.

It shouldn't be so hard.

'Hey, man, sorry.' Roy said.

Roy had lost his lower legs and his good looks in that bomb blast. He was a father and a husband, and he didn't want to live. He'd made it clear to Micky on the first day he'd met him. 'Why didn't they let me die? I wanted to die?' he'd asked Micky.

Micky had no answer for him.

'Fuck this,' Roy said. 'Let's go see the world.'

Roy began pushing the wheels on his chair. The road led to a sandy cove, to a family picnic where Roy's wife and child waited for them. In his wheelchair on a sandy beach, Roy pushed the wheels as hard as he could, but it tipped forward, propelling him face-first into the sand. He pushed Micky's hands away as he tried to help him.

'Daddy …' A little boy a bit older than Mia came running across the sand. Micky straightened up the wheelchair and helped Roy back into it.

'Hey, Tiger, how you doing?' Roy said.

He pulled the little boy up onto his knees and hugged him to his chest.

The little boy stared at Micky and said, 'Who are you?'

'This is my friend Mike,' Roy said. 'Mike, this is Scotty.'

The little boy held out his hand and said, 'How do you do, Mike.'

Micky gathered the pieces of his heart back together and put a smile on his face. 'How do you do, Scotty,' he said as he held the little hand.

Roy's wife Janet came across the sand, her eyes locked on Micky. He turned his face away and concentrated on Roy. Between them, they tugged the chair to the shade of the umbrella covering the picnic blanket. The little boy ran down to the water's edge.

'Can I swim Mummy?' he asked.

'Don't go too deep,' she said.

'Coming in, Daddy?' he asked.

Micky and Roy had pulled a car tyre to pieces; had taken the inner tube out and inflated it so Roy could spend time in the water with his son. Micky helped Roy out of the wheelchair and into the tyre, his little boy looking on until Roy paddled around in the water with his boy.

Micky and Janet sat on the blanket and watched.

'I'm sorry,' she said.

Micky didn't know what to say. It wasn't okay and he wasn't going to say that. He did understand she was lonely and afraid, and she'd had too much to drink, but it wasn't okay.

The family barbeque: another one of those things you take for granted until it's taken away from you. Held at Janet's parents' home, the backyard pool sparkled. Micky had a swim and was getting changed from the t-shirt he always wore into a dry shirt. Janet had come into the cabana. She was a pretty woman, with dark hair, dark eyes, lonely and afraid. She'd put her arms around his neck, seeking his mouth. It had startled him. He'd pulled her arms away, looked her in the eyes and said, 'I can't.'

'Roy doesn't care,' she'd said.

He'd walked away shaken. Had he been flirty with her? He hadn't thought so, but he had enjoyed her company while sharing a drink and talking about her family and Roy.

Janet reached out and put her hand on his arm. He looked into her eyes.

'He doesn't care,' she said. 'He doesn't even want to stay alive for us.' They both looked at the little boy swimming with his father.

'You can't say that,' Micky said. But he'd said those words only the other night: *Emmy would be better off if I was dead*. Did he think that?

'I don't care anymore. I'm tired, I'm lonely, I want someone to hold me. Someone to love me,' Janet said.

'I can't do that,' Micky said.

'He doesn't care.'

Micky was drowning.

'I can't love you,' he said.

He turned his eyes away so she shouldn't see into his heart, his memories. He was trying to tell her; he couldn't tell her.

'I don't mind. I just want someone to hold me.'

'I mind,' he said.

He rose from the blanket and walked down to the water's edge. *Emmy.*

Janet joined him. His body was stiff, holding himself together.

'You have someone you love,' she said.

'Yes.' *Stop talking!* He didn't want to do this.

'She's lucky,' Janet said and splashed into the water, calling her son's name, her husband's eyes on her and Micky.

Lucky? Cruel and selfish, his father had said.

Chapter Twenty-five

August 1974

Emmaline

Denim jeans rolled up to her knees, Emmy sat on a concrete river embankment, dipping her toes towards the water. She pushed the sleeves of her blue blouse up and leant back, turning her face towards the hot sun.

People snuggled together under trees and on the grass or exposed their skin to the sun. Couples strolled arm in arm in the warm breeze that blew off the river. Sunshine sparkled on waves as it chased the wake of a little open-top boat putting past her.

Emmy was in Paris.

'Emmaline.'

She heard her name. Emmy turned to the voice. 'Sister Mary-Anne,' she said.

'Just Mary-Anne,' was the reply.

Emmy stood and wrapped her arms around the woman who had seemed so old when she had first met her. The woman she owed so much to held her tight then pushed her away to look at her.

'Mary-Anne?' Emmy queried.

Then she noticed the missing Nun's habit, the hair that had grown into a short dark bob, the denim flares and the floral blouse. The years that had disappeared.

'Mummy!' her daughter called. They turned to see Mia coming towards them, swinging between two men.

'You found your young man then?' Mary-Anne said.

Emmy and Mary-Anne studied the scene before them. Mia, almost five, dressed in a pink and white Petite Battue striped dress, swinging between Jacob, dressed in checked flares and a plain blue linen shirt, and Peter, dressed in dark blue flares and a light blue silk shirt. Jacob's beret perched sideways over his blond hair. Peter carried an ice cream that was melting in the sun and dripping down the sleeve of his silk shirt. Jacob tried to hide his amusement at Peter's discomfort, and Peter tried not to let his discomfort spill over.

Emmy turned her gaze back to Mary-Anne, and they both burst into giggles.

'Maybe not,' Mary-Anne said.

'I did find him,' Emmy said. She could talk about Micky now; she could get some words out. 'But he had to go away.'

'I'm sorry,' Mary-Anne said.

'Yes.'

Introductions were made. Mia took her ice cream from Peter and sat on the embankment, swinging her legs. Peter took out his handkerchief and wiped the ice cream off his arm and shirt sleeve. Jacob burst into laughter and Peter tossed the dirty cloth at him.

'You can make your way home?' Jacob asked Emmy.

'Yes, I can. Down the Avenue then left onto Rue De Rivoli and right on Rue Saint-Roch, four doors down, open the gate up the steps. I'll be okay. You guys go.'

Emmy watched them walk away, their arms around each other, Peter resting his head on Jacob's shoulder. They were in Paris, *the City of Love*. If they couldn't do that here, where could they do it?

'What have you been doing, Emmaline?' Mary-Anne asked.

'Emmy ... please call me Emmy or Em.' *Micky calls me Emmaline.* 'Mia is nearly five. We are living in London with the boys.'

'That's where you went when you left the Home.'

'Yes.' Emmy remembered the cold and being hungry. 'Yes, but we moved back there before Christmas last year. We are in Paris on holiday; I will be going home soon.' There was so much to tell, but she said, 'What about you? You left the church?'

'Yes, I needed time to think. I'm working with orphans in Vietnam now.'

Emmy's heart missed a beat at that word. *Vietnam*, where she'd lost Micky.

'Are you still teaching?' Mary-Anne asked her.

Teaching … it had been a long time since Emmy had done any teaching. She shook her head. 'Maybe when I get home.'

'You must, Emmy. It's what you worked hard for.'

'Yes.' She had worked hard, but since Mia's birth, *her* needs had come first, and then on the Kibbutz, her work was allocated to her. She had done some teaching there.

'I'm in Paris interviewing at the Loreto Convent. I need a teacher for the orphanage. I haven't found anyone I'm happy with yet. I could use your help if you are looking for an opportunity to teach,' Mary-Anne said.

Vietnam. Emmy wasn't sure. 'Is it safe?' she asked.

'Yes. We are in Saigon. A peace treaty was signed in 1973.'

Emmy knew that. That was how Micky had come home to her. She also knew how Micky had been treated, or what he had told her. He didn't need words though; she had seen the scars on his body.

Emmy and Mary-Anne spent the afternoon chatting and reminiscing while Mia ran around on the grass, tumbling and doing handstands or resting her head on her mother's knee. Emmy shared the picnic she'd prepared for the boys with Mary-Anne, surprised when she enjoyed a glass of wine with her. Time went by. The sun moved west and soon it was time to say goodbye.

'I'll be here for another week.' Mary-Anne said. 'Saigon is safe – the Australian government has an Embassy there. And the government of South Vietnam approves our orphanage. There are many children who need our help.'

Two days later, Emmy stood in front of an elegant building on the Rue Auguste Comte. Jacob's nerves were tangible; she could feel his body tremble as he stood beside her.

'It's okay. She won't bite,' Peter said as he put his arm around Jacob.

Today, Peter was introducing Jacob, the man he loved, to his grandmother. That had surprised Emmy, that Peter's grandmother knew and had accepted him for who he was. And it had been more of a surprise when Peter had addressed his grandmother as The Countess.

Emmy was nervous too. She'd never met a countess, but her heart went out to Jacob. Here they were, two children of refugees, dressed in their best clothing. Jacob had upgraded most of his clothes, with Peter's help, shopping in Carnaby Street, and he looked wonderful. His blond hair was longer, just above his collar. He wore his cap sitting at an angle, his paisley silk shirt tucked into denim flares. He had a long scarf tucked into the pocket of the leather bomber jacket that sat over his shoulder.

Emmy wore a frock she'd bought from Galeries Lafayette in Paris, also with Peter's help, a bit more daring than her usual style. Of pale blue silk, it wrapped around her body, had a low neckline that she kept tugging at, a tight waist and a flowing skirt that rested just above her knees. She wore wedged sandals and, at Peter's insistence, a crocheted hat over her shoulder-length bob.

And Peter, she should have guessed by the way he dressed – the shirts he wore, his shoes, everything about him – cried out 'wealthy'. But she had been so happy for Jacob, she hadn't noticed.

Now Emmy and Jacob stood on the steps of the Villa Saint Michele, the Paris residence of the Countess Paulette de Caron; she had left Mia in the care of Mary-Anne.

Peter pushed the front doorbell.

'What did you tell her about me?' Jacob asked.

'That I love you, and I want to spend the rest of my life with you,' Peter said.

'Oh.' Emmy couldn't hide her delight as she put her hands to her mouth.

Jacob reached around the back of Peter's neck, pulled him close and said, 'Yes.'

The front door opened.

'Bienvenue à la maison jeune maître,' a grey-haired man said as he opened the door.

'Il est bon de vous voir, Maurice,' Peter said.

The room they were shown into was just like Emmy imagined, a setting in an old Hollywood movie. The colours were deep and dark, burgundy and blues; tapestry hanging on the wall; brocade-covered furniture; a table set with silver. Pictures of family members on the wall. She didn't belong here, and she could see Jacob's uncertainty about where he would fit.

'I love you,' Peter whispered as he pulled Jacob close.

Jacob nodded.

Emmy moved away to give them space of their own. She drifted around the room, looking at the photographs on display. Looking at a picture of two men in uniform, her body trembled. Her heart raced, and she reached out to pick up the picture.

'Don't touch that,' a voice behind her said in English. Emmy turned to face the speaker.

'Who are you?' she was asked.

'Papa,' Emmy whispered.

But it wasn't her father; it was an older version of him. White hair bundled on top of her head, back straight, shoulders back, wearing a navy Chanel suit, not a male but a female version of him. The Countess de Caron entered the room, her stick clattering on the floor. She stood in front of Emmy, staring into her face.

'Who are you?'

'Grandmother, this is Emmaline, my friend,' Peter said.

Emmy glanced from Peter to the photograph. 'Who are they?' she asked.

'My father and his younger brother. I am named after him. They died in the war.'

'Jacob!' Emmy reached out, and he held her hand. Then he looked at the photograph.

'Shit, Emmy, it can't be,' he said.

'John Peter Cannon. My father is John Peter Cannon,' Emmy said.

But she knew her father had been in the French Army, knew his name wouldn't have always been John Peter. Like Peter's name, it would have a French interpretation. Emmy has seen that picture before. Like the photograph of Mama, hidden, tucked away in a corner. She would never have seen it if she hadn't been helping her father with the twins, her parents' lives hidden from her and her brothers. Papa wouldn't tell her anything about it.

But he had told her before she went to Melbourne; he had told her his family had turned him out, his family in France. His first baby, her brother, had died.

'I have to go,' Emmy said.

Jacob held her hand. 'I'll come with you,' he said. His eyes on Peter, the love and confusion colliding.

'No, Jacob. Stay with Peter. He loves you.' She kissed Jacob on the cheek and walked towards the door, one step at a time, her legs like lead. She passed the old lady who turned her head away, passed Peter who looked more confused than she was. The old man opened the door, and she was outside. She took a deep breath, wiped her eyes, straightened her skirt and staggered down the steps onto the street.

Chapter Twenty-six

August 1974

Micky

Micky and Roy sat fishing, sharing the quiet companionship men enjoyed without the need for unnecessary chatter. Micky hadn't fished for many years; it was a pleasure he'd shared with his father but only after his sister Jessica grew older. Fishing had been her special time with their father.

Micky and Roy had been fishing before, but they had never caught any fish, and he didn't expect today to be any different. That was how most of the fishing trips had gone over his life: hours spent sitting, pulling bait off a line and putting bait back on the line. The fish were never in danger. As he grew older, his father no longer went to sea, his grandmother passed away, and the family moved back to San Francisco. He grew older still; went away to college, and the fishing trips became rarer.

On this hot summer's day at the end of August, a gentle wind blew over the water, ruffling up the waves. Gulls squawked in the clear blue sky; boats of all shapes and sizes moved across the bay. The Golden Gate Bridge stood tall and proud between the landmasses to the left of the jetty.

Tomorrow Micky was taking Roy for the first fitting of his prosthesis. As this day had approached, Roy became more agitated.

'What's your girl's name?' Roy asked.

'Emmaline,' he said before he realised. She was always there, always in his mind. Some days he could push her away, most days he couldn't.

'How …?' Micky asked.

He'd never told Roy about Emmy. He'd never spoken about her to anyone. Not during all the time he'd spent in Mexico talking and trying to make sense of what had happened to him. Not to anyone, if he could avoid it.

He knew what he was doing to her, what he was doing to himself. He had to keep Emmy safe.

'I have eyes, Mike. I can see. Janet needs a whole man. She's pretty … fun to be with … I can see what's going on.'

'I never …'

'I know.'

Roy's fishing line tugged at his hand. He wound the reel, bringing the catch out of the water onto the jetty. The fish fell off the hook and floundered around at their feet, struggling for life. They watched, like two little boys unsure of what to do.

'Put it back,' they said together. 'Put it back.'

Micky scooped up the squirming creature and dropped it as gently as he could back into the water.

The next day they were back on the jetty. The trip to the doctors had gone as Micky expected. Roy had struggled with his artificial limbs, his agitation not helped by a well-meant comment that 'it takes time to get used to these changes'.

A summer storm was blowing in over the bay, making the water choppy and murky. Roy tipped his wheelchair forward and pushed himself into the water. Micky stood stunned; it took him time to register what was happening. He heard Janet and Scotty yelling from behind him as he took off his shoes and dived into the water.

He couldn't see Roy, the current pulling him, tugging him down deep. His eyes stung, his lungs were bursting, so he had to surface. Janet and Scotty were crying on the jetty. He took a breath and dived again, stopped struggling with the flow of the water and let it carry him.

Why? But he understood why. This couldn't happen again; he couldn't let someone else die.

He needed to breathe; he needed to surface again. *A shadow in the water.* He saw Roy floating; saw Roy change his mind. Roy struggled against the ocean but failed. Sank deeper.

Micky gasped for air and grabbed him; he held Roy's head above the surface.

'Don't let me go,' Roy spluttered.

'I won't.'

Micky struggled towards the shore, dragging Roy with him. A small crowd had gathered and, as he stumbled over the stone embankment, someone took Roy out of his grip and helped him over the stones; helped him across the road to the lawn and sat him on the grass. Micky could hear sirens in the background; saw Janet and Scotty running to Roy.

The ambulance arrived and the first aid attendants ran to Roy. Micky fell onto the grassed area, his lungs heaving in more air, his eyes focused. He watched the scene playing out in front of him like a slow-motion movie. Ambulance attendants leant over Roy, covering his face with a mask, lifting him onto a stretcher.

'Daddy, Daddy,' Scotty cried.

Roy removed the mask and said in a weak voice, 'I'm okay, Scotty. Daddy was very silly to fall off the jetty like that.'

Scotty was lifted onto the stretcher and Roy wrapped his arms around his son. Janet stood beside the stretcher holding Roy's hand. She glanced at Micky and whispered, 'Thank you.'

As Roy was wheeled into the ambulance, a shadow fell over Micky; a hand rested on his back, and a towel wrapped around his shoulders.

'You okay, buddy?'

Am I okay? 'Yes,' he said.

That night Micky wrote a letter.

Chapter Twenty-seven

October 1974

Emmaline.

Emmy received a letter. Tears ran down her face as she read it. Sweat trickled between her breasts, dampening her white blouse. She ran her hands through her hair, damp from the humidity, but at least it wasn't in her face anymore.

The day after she arrived in Saigon, the first thing Emmy did was find a hairdresser; had her hair cut short, like Twiggy's 1968 style. She did the same with Mia's hair but left it longer, so she had a little crop of dark curls covering her head. Then she'd gone shopping for suitable clothing – cotton and silk tunics and shift dresses, a western version of clothing the local girls and ladies wore – her European clothing too heavy for the climate, or unsuitable for the culture. That had been two weeks ago, on Mia's fifth birthday. Sometimes it felt like she'd been born yesterday, and other times it felt like an eternity away from her father.

I promise I will do everything I can to make it right, Peter had written.

He had been more confused than her. Emmy should have noticed, but his accent and his love for Jacob had distracted her. She always thought Mia saw Micky in Peter, but now she knew Mia had seen her grandfather, her Opa, in him.

The day after she'd met his grandmother, *her* grandmother, they had shared coffee at the Café Domenico on the Rue du 29

Juillet. He'd told her, 'My mother married a GI at the end of the war, and we went to live in San Diego. I was seven. He was a kind man and adopted me and gave me his name. He died in the Korean war. After that, my mother struggled. I tried to help her, but she started drinking, seeing men. One she settled with. I was getting older, more confused. He didn't like me.' He'd stopped talking, recollection in his eyes. Emmy held his hand.

'I grew up; understood who I was. My grandmother, *our* grandmother, surprised me when she invited me back home, when she accepted me for who I am. I was always told my father and his brother, your father, had died in the war.'

Emmy read on.

> *I have always thought I was alone, that after Grandmother there would only be me. I hope you understand how wonderful it is for me to find out that is not the case.*
>
> *Grandmother will not talk about your father, only to say he died in the war. And she has said it so many times she now believes it to be the truth. It was thirty years ago but for her, it is as if time has stood still. She is not unkind, the war affected her, as it did so many, and I don't think she will ever forget or forgive, but I hope you can.*
>
> *Jacob is missing you and Mia, as am I.*
>
> *Write to us and tell us all your adventures. Be careful and keep safe.*
>
> *Your loving cousin, Peter.*

My cousin Peter. She might have noticed if she'd been looking. She only had scraps of information from her father. He had always said, 'We look forward, Emmy. We move forward.' He never wanted to talk about the past.

Emmy folded the letter and returned it to the envelope.

Yes, she could forgive, but she hadn't gone back home to her family. What could she say to her parents? She had sent Papa a letter telling him she was working in an orphanage, teaching. She had sent him the address and told him not to worry; it was safe for her and Mia to be in Saigon, and she hoped she was right.

Mia had cried on the plane. Jacob was the man she had called Papa for much of her life, and he was a man Emmy would always love. He had given her so much; she loved him and shared his happiness. But he had found the person he would love for the rest of his life, the person he deserved, his life partner. Emmy hoped one day Jacob and Peter could be more than that to each other, and she would move on, look after Mia, and find a life of her own.

As the flight came into Saigon, Emmy saw rice fields and jungles covering the ground. She also saw evidence of a war that had raged for more than thirty years. Mary-Anne met them at the airport, and they travelled by taxi through the hot, crowded streets. The only moving air came through the open windows, strange exotic aromas wafting on that breeze, mixed with the familiar aroma of French bread and coffee.

Mary-Anne had a spare room in her apartment, which she made available to Emmy and Mia. It was within walking distance of the orphanage but seemed miles away. The apartment could have been on the outskirts of Paris. The white building sat on a tree-lined boulevard. Double, black doors at the front entrance opened into a courtyard. A staircase led to the upper floors, the apartment Emmy would share on the first floor. Inside, she could have been back in Paris, the chic white furniture, all the modern appliances, even a television. There was a view from the kitchen window of the cobble-paved central courtyard where flowers grew on trellises along the walls. Emmy's surprise must have shown.

Mary-Anne said, 'I don't own the apartment. It belongs to

Chien Tran; his family business has been involved with the orphanage for many years. The western girls who work at the orphanage live here.'

Adjusting to the climate, the humidity and the heat took time, but Emmy was grateful she wasn't in the cold of London. The noise and the traffic were not unlike London, but completely different – smaller, faster and constant. Pushbikes were everywhere. London was chaos, but it seemed organised chaos. Saigon was just chaos. She knew it would take time to work it out.

On Friday, the 18th of October, Emmy and Mia walked along Le Lai, a road or street, Emmy wasn't sure – she called it a boulevard. Shops and businesses on one side and open space on the other. School was finished for the day, and Emmy had bought groceries from the market and was making her way home. Sweat poured down Emmy's shirt, her hair was damp, and her backpack clung to her. Mia dragged on her arm.

'Come on, Mia, we have to hurry,' Emmy said.

'Mummy …'

The sky was growing dark as a storm raced towards the city. Thunder rumbled in the distance and the lightning was getting brighter.

'We have to hurry.'

Emmy knew she had to reach the apartment before the storm broke. She'd never seen a storm like this: the sky swirled in shades of grey and black, and clouds raced towards her. Cars rushed by with headlights on. Pedestrians hurried, pushing into her on their way past. Then the sky above her went black, and damp air enclosed her. Emmy was the only one on the street. Where had everyone gone!

'Emmaline.'

Mia turned to the voice and cried, 'Daddy.'

Emmy froze.

Lightning split the sky, crackled. And thunder roared. Mia screamed at its closeness, and Emmy's legs went weak. Strong hands were there to steady her.

'Where are you going?' he asked.

'Home,' Emmy replied, waving her arm in the direction she'd been walking. Lightning hit the ground ahead of her, and she ducked and threw her body over Mia. Her eyes blinded, her hair prickling, thunder echoed in her ears. The air sizzled, the acrid smell of burning tainted the space around her. The wind began to blow. Then rain fell. Ice cold rain. Almost hail.

Mia sobbed, and when he picked her up, she clung to him.

'Hush, hush, I've got you,' he said as he patted her back gently. 'Come on now.'

He steadied Emmy, turned her around and led her into a café, where he slipped off her backpack and sat her on a red vinyl bench at a green laminex table. Lowering Mia to her lap, he went and ordered drinks: brandy for her, whisky for him. He then slid onto the bench opposite her.

Wind battered the building, tossing rubbish at the glass windows, which shook and twisted. Lightning hit the ground nearby and rain poured until waterfalls cascaded off the tin roof. The hot air turned cold. Emmy shivered, and Mia huddled in her arms; she spoke soothing words to calm her, to calm herself.

Emmy stared into brown eyes.

But it wasn't Micky who sat opposite her: it was his father.

He sipped his drink as she stared at him.

Micky's father. But her last letter wouldn't have reached him yet. The letter with pictures of Mia on her birthday, on an aeroplane heading to Saigon. Her letter telling him of her plans to work in an orphanage, teaching children, telling him she'd been advised it was safe for her and Mia to be in Saigon, that the peace pact was in force. These things he would already know.

And she had told him she was excited to be helping children who needed so much.

'What are you doing here?' he asked.

'Working. I'm working. I wrote …' Emmy stopped speaking. She didn't have to explain to Michael Brannigan what she was doing. She didn't need his permission.

He held up his hand. 'You don't have to explain to me.'

'I know.'

She wanted to ask him … wanted to say, 'Where is Micky? What's happening to him? When will I see him?' But she didn't. She said, 'I didn't understand when I came here … I know the orphanage I work at is well run and the children are cared for. But so many children have no one to look after them … I didn't understand …'

He reached across the table and placed his hand over hers. She missed her father and turned her hand to hold his, to take comfort from him. She sipped her brandy and warmed up as the storm outside raged, ripping the roof off the building next door and tearing up trees in the park opposite.

Mia curled into her chest, glancing at the man sitting opposite her.

'I will be in Saigon for some time,' Michael said. 'Kate will be joining me soon. Will you visit us?'

Nothing about Micky. Not a word about him. She had always respected their wishes and would continue to do so. She said, 'I would like that.'

Chapter Twenty-eight

Emmaline

The next day a knock came on the door.

Mary-Anne opened it and said, 'Oh.' Then she said, 'Emmy, there's someone to see you. Come on, Mia. Let's go for a walk.'

Mia left her drawing, took Mary-Anne's outstretched hand and left the apartment.

Emmy stood at the door, numb. A soldier stood before her, a soldier dressed in khaki, clutching his cap.

Micky stood before her.

He reached out. She stepped back, away from his touch, away from the heartbreak.

Micky

Micky saw Mia peek over her shoulder, her backward glances checking him out as she reached the top of the staircase. Now Emmy stepped away from his touch. He didn't know what he had expected, but not that. His letter, the one he'd written after leaving her with no word from him for more than a year, had come back unopened. He knew Emmy hadn't received it; knew she hadn't sent it back unopened.

'May I come in?' he asked.

Emmy stepped aside and allowed him access to the room. She left him standing, looking around the apartment while she went into the alcove that contained the kitchen. He saw her lean against the workbench, lift her hand to her face, straighten her back before she opened the fridge.

The room had a table and four chairs. A television sat on a cabinet on the far wall. On a coffee table in front of a blue and green brocade couch, he saw a pink photo album. On the cover, in a child's handwriting, it said: *Mia's family*. He knew he shouldn't pick it up, shouldn't look inside, but he did.

Inside, on the first page, was that picture – the picture taken by a stranger on a sunny winter's day on the Fremantle Esplanade – him, Mia and Emmy. Emmy had written under each person: Daddy, Mia, Mummy.

On the opposite page was a picture of Jacob with his arm around another man. Emmy had written: Jacob and Peter.

It would have surprised him if Mia had recognised him. He'd hardly recognised himself: he was skin over bones, his eyes hollow, his hair long and shaggy; a stick rested beside him. But Emmy he could see, though it was under makeup, the bruises on her face, the cut on her lip. He'd done that, and staying away was all he could do to keep her safe. Could she forgive him?

The glasses tinkled on the tray. He put the book down, took the tray from Emmy, and they sat on the couch. She stared at the blank television on the far wall; sat away from him, not next to him, not where he thought she would be.

'It's too hot for coffee,' she said and picked up the jug. The lemonade spilled over the side.

'Yes,' he said and took the jug.

She moved her hand away from his. He poured the drinks.

Had he been cruel and selfish? He could have killed Emmy that night if his father hadn't come home when he had. He had decided to keep Emmy safe; he'd made that decision. Was he right to do that, or was he … *selfish*?

His nightmares still hounded him, but he understood they were nightmares, a memory of the past. He could not let them control his future. The time he'd spent with Roy and Janet had helped him, showing him that what had happened to him was not who he was, who he could be. He did not have to let his past destroy him.

His mother was right. He couldn't leave Emmy without any word from him. That was *cruel and selfish*. Emmy and Mia were his family. But had he left it too long?

His trembling hand reached out to her. Emmy pulled back away from his touch.

'Don't,' she said. 'Please, Micky, I'm almost alright without you. Almost alright. Don't touch me if you can't stay.'

'Forever?' he asked.

'Forever.'

Emmy moved along the couch into his arms, where she should be. Where she had been on those lonely dark nights, on the days when he was starving, on the days when his body and mind screamed with pain, where if she hadn't been, he would have died. He turned her face to his, wiped her tears away, and closed his eyes as he put his lips to hers.

Chapter Twenty-nine

Micky

Two weeks later, Micky drove a car he'd borrowed from his father as he'd done when he was a teenager. His girlfriend cuddled up beside him as he drove through the streets of Saigon; he felt eighteen years old again. He took his hand from the steering wheel; put it over Emmy's shoulder and down the front of her blouse; she didn't stop him.

Eighteen years old; before he'd gone to war; before he'd had to grow up. They had left Mia with her grandparents.

He asked her, 'Do you have a swimsuit.'

'Why?'

'I have the keys to a private beach.'

'How can you have a private beach?' Emmy said. 'There'd be a riot at home if such a thing was to happen.'

He shrugged. He didn't know who owned the beach and didn't care. His father had arranged it for him, and it was his and Emmy's for the day. He'd only seen her once for a short time since the day in her apartment. He'd been on duty for the past two weeks; now he had a day off to spend with her.

Emmy had packed a picnic.

A white lace blouse and a pair of extremely short red shorts covered the multi-coloured bikini Emmy wore – clothing, as a respectable girl, she could never have worn in public in Saigon. Her short hair had been a surprise; it made *her* look eighteen again.

He wore dark shorts and a white t-shirt – ordinary civilian

clothes. They were teenagers on a date.

The drive was long. With the city behind them, they drove through outer villages, past banana plantations and then through rice fields as they headed towards the jungle, the hills and the ocean. It gave them time together to talk, to sit, to learn about each other. He told her about his stay in Mexico, but only what he wanted her to know.

'The aircrews were more experienced, had training on what to expect as prisoners. We hadn't, but even they struggled.'

'Micky.'

He told her about his work with Roy – didn't tell her everything about Roy

Emmy hesitated, her eyes filled with tears. When he noticed, he found a spot to park the car and pulled over. She curled into his body, trembling. After holding her for a time, he eased her away and said, 'Tell me.'

Emmy told him about the attack on the Kibbutz, and he saw her failed attempt to keep the fear and terror from her face. He couldn't breathe. His heart pounded, and he was tearing apart.

'Emmy.' He pulled her back into his arms, into his body, ran his fingers through her hair and kissed her forehead. 'I'm sorry. You shouldn't have been there. I should have protected you. I'm sorry.'

Then Emmy pushed away from his arms, took his face in her hands and looked into his eyes. 'Don't ever say that, Micky. Don't ever say you are sorry. You had to do what you did. I know you had to.'

She was protecting him, protecting him when he should have protected her. He loved Emmy. She was the reason he was alive but, until that moment, he hadn't realised how much she loved him. She had accepted that he'd made decisions for her, to protect himself; she'd understood why. She'd stayed away, giving him the time and space he'd needed. She'd shielded him, protected him, loved him.

He gulped down his terror; held himself tight; breathed and slowed his heart rate: all the things he'd been taught to do. He couldn't let her know the dread inside him. He understood what his father had tried to tell him, that he could have lost Emmy and Mia. How would he have survived that?

He held Emmy in his arms, breathed in her scent, her essence. She was safe, in his arms. Mia was safe, with his parents.

Micky put his lips to Emmy's and caressed her mouth, and she wrapped herself around him. Sweat trickled between them in the hot car, the open windows offering no breeze. They pulled apart. There were other cars on the road, civilian and military vehicles passing by. Occasionally one would slow, and a head would pop out of a window asking if they were okay; he would wave them on.

'William's ship was in port. He was working at the medical post,' Emmy said. 'He helped us, and Jacob looked after us.'

He flinched at Jacob's name.

Emmy told him about Peter. 'They are so happy together. I am so happy for Jacob.'

'I'm happy for him too.' he said, and he was.

Now that note made sense. He could never repay Jacob for all he'd done.

He told her he had written to her, that his letter had come back; he didn't tell her Jacob had written a note with the returned letter.

'I could have gone back on board the Jackson, but she would have taken me away from you. There was an opportunity to join the Security Guard in Saigon.' he said.

'I never received the letter.' Emmy said.

He knew. He also knew the reason he hadn't gone back on board the Jackson was because of the note Jacob had written.

Emmy and Mia have gone to Saigon. Emmy is teaching

*at Sacred Heart Orphanage. I hope they will be safe, and
I hope you will find each other. Jacob.*

He was ready to drive again.

Emmaline

Emmy had never received the letter, so didn't know what it said, but it wasn't important now. She was in Micky's arms, where she should be.

She saw him holding himself tight, pushing the darkness away after she told him about the Kibbutz. He had to know she was safe here with him. Mia was safe. He could not take any blame for the attack on the Kibbutz; she would not allow that.

Micky drove the car back onto the road while Emmy told him about her trip to Berlin, about her mother's sisters, that Jacob had not been able to find his sister. 'We didn't stay long it was a cold and sad place.'

She told him of her plans to return home, but after meeting Peter's grandmother, her grandmother … 'I couldn't go home, not yet. Mary-Anne offered me work in the orphanage; I thought I could help.'

Micky squeezed her shoulder.

The drive came to an end at a gate on a dirt road. Jungle surrounded the track, and trees blocked any breeze. Hot, damp, humid air dripped off the leaves, wetting their skin and clothes. The dirt track led through the trees, where insect noise and bird song floated in the air. Emmy heard the surf breaking before she felt the breeze blow in off the ocean. Then the track opened onto a beach, and the damp air was left behind, the jungle giving way to coastal rocks that protected the area from prying eyes.

At the beach, a small blue and white coloured building sat on manicured grass lawns. A sun shelter, covered in palm leaves, stood beside the building. The white sands appeared to have been raked clean. It could have been a beach in the south of France, except for the humidity. Micky laid towels under the shelter and Emmy set the picnic basket down.

When they'd finished eating, Emmy opened a glass dish and burst into laughter.

'What?' he said.

'It's supposed to be chocolate-covered strawberries.'

In the bowl was a mush of melted chocolate with strawberries floating around.

'It's supposed to be a sexy sweet, to tease you with,' Emmy said.

'A sexy sweet to tease me …'

'Yes.'

What a silly idea. It was too hot for anything like that. Emmy lowered her eyes, but Micky lifted her chin and looked into her eyes.

Micky

Micky's hands shook. He'd made love with Emmy only three times, but he remembered her body and the way it curved into his, the way he'd felt knowing he was the first man she'd made love with. The purity of her lovemaking was so unlike the business transactions he'd had in Mexico when he'd been out having drinks with the guys. He was always left feeling soiled and frustrated.

His fingers fumbled with the buttons on her blouse, but Emmy steadied his hand, helped him open the buttons, then she ran her fingers down to his shorts. He didn't remember much after that; the urgency they both had when making love muddled his thoughts. Then he realised Emmy, lying beside him, had tears on her face. He stroked her cheek.

'Don't leave me again, Micky,' she said.

'I won't,' he promised.

The first time he'd made love with Emmy was before he'd gone to war when they were both young and innocent. The second was after he'd come back, after he knew about cruelty and pain, after his innocence had been stripped from him. On that night …

He pushed those thoughts away, still grateful his father had come home when he had.

He missed Emmy. He missed the memory of her, the innocence of her, his reason to live, the reason he stayed alive.

He rolled onto his elbow and studied her body. Her clothing was dishevelled, her shirt open. She still wore her bikini top, but her shorts and bikini bottom were on the towel with his shorts. He could do better than that.

'Let me,' he said.

He removed her shirt, dipped his fingers into the melted chocolate and ran them down between her breasts. Flicking open the catch on her bikini top, he made his way around her body with chocolate-covered fingers. Then he bent his head and followed the line of chocolate with his mouth.

Emmaline

Emmy remembered Micky running his fingers around her breasts, down her stomach, between her legs. She remembered his mouth following his fingers; she remembered pulling him into her, holding his body, him holding hers, never wanting the moment to end. But it had to, and now his naked body draped around her, his heart beating fast. She was hot and sweaty and now covered in chocolate. He rolled away from her, and Emmy turned to face him, her heartbeat slowing, her breathing becoming steadier.

Emmy sucked in air and said, 'Oh …'

'You are amazing,' he said and wiped chocolate from her face with the back of his hand.

The laughter on his face, the love in his eyes, Emmy knew no one would ever love her as Micky did, and she knew she didn't want anyone but Micky to love her like this.

'Marry me?' he asked.

She nodded.

'I'm supposed to get on one knee, give you a ring in a little felt box, not ask you like this,' he said. He was smiling, but she could see his concern.

'I love you, Micky. I don't need a ring in a little felt box.' No, she didn't need a ring in a felt box; she didn't need him to fall on one knee and ask her. She would marry him, and they would be together, forever.

He drew her over his body, and she straddled him, her eyes staring at the scars on his chest. He took her face in his hands and pulled her down, him kissing her face and eyes blotting out the image.

Later, Emmy lay on her back, looking up through the thatched roof to the sky. She held Micky's hand as they watched clouds scud by, the blue sky now grey. Rain began to fall.

'Come on, let's get washed,' Micky said. He pulled her up and they ran into the ocean, he thinner than he should be, the scars on his back breaking her heart. She had to know he was home, he was safe, he was here, with her, and always would be. She followed him into the ocean.

Chapter Thirty

Emmaline

When she had first arrived at the orphanage, Emmy had cried most nights after Mia was asleep and she was alone. The children at the Sacred Heart Orphanage were of mixed races, children whose fathers had returned to the USA or Australia, most never knowing they had a child. The children could not be unnoticed. They were different. The stigma and shame of having a mixed-race child saw these children abandoned as their mothers tried to live a life away from poverty and disgrace.

The three-storey Sacred Heart Orphanage sat on a crowded street. The rent from the street frontage shops helped provide funds for the work the orphanage did. Upstairs on the first and second floor, the business of looking after the children went on. The staff were six westerners, including Emmy, two French Sisters of Loreto trained in mothercraft, and two Vietnamese Sisters of Loreto trained in mothercraft. Four local ladies, who also looked after the children, cooked and clean. Two of these ladies helped interpret local customs and laws. An older man who had suffered injuries in the war tended the garden and drove the bus when needed. At night three grandmothers, older ladies, slept with the children in the dormitories. They shared food with the children and had the use of washing facilities, the buildings and gardens during the day. Without Mary-Anne's help, these ladies would have been sleeping on the street.

The first floor held the dining and living area for the children, as well as a staff room and a classroom. The next floor contained the dormitories. As the children grew, the nursery got smaller, the boys' and girls' rooms bigger. Bathroom facilities were on both floors. Outside, behind the building, was a garden for playing and growing vegetables.

Mary-Anne had been the orphanage administrator since mid-1971. The number of mixed-race children had declined since the withdrawal of the Australian troops in 1971 and the US troops in 1973. Many of the children were now older and harder to place with adoptive families. Mary-Anne worked with the US group *Friends for All Children* and the *Australian Adoptive Families Association*.

'Give it some time,' she'd said when Emmy told her it was time for her to go home, that she was sorry: she'd thought she was stronger, braver.

'You were there when Mia was born. If it hadn't been for you … if I hadn't had Michael and Kate, I wouldn't have Mia.'

'I know.'

Emmy dried her eyes and held Mary-Anne's hand. 'Isn't there anything we can do to help the mothers keep their children?' she asked.

'We can try. We hope one day we will be able to do more, have a place where we can teach the mothers skills and help them with financial support. But we can only do our best for the children and hope we can find them a loving family because there are many families looking for children to love.'

'Yes,' Emmy said. She knew the children would be loved and supported. She had to believe that. She understood most mothers who gave away a child didn't have the opportunity she had. Sometimes at night, that frightened her. How would she have lived if she'd never seen Mia, never held her, never been her mother? Would it be like the counsellor had said … a memory in time as the years go by, like a death. But it wasn't a death – it was a life, and there would be the aching. Did you do the right thing?

What happened to the child? Was the child happy, cared for, loved? Did the child forgive you? You had to answer yes, knowing there was no other choice, like the mothers who left their children in the orphanage.

'You are braver than you think,' Mary-Anne told her.

Emmy did her best for the children and their mothers. She decorated the walls of her classroom with pictures and made space for the children's drawings. The furniture was old but sturdy, where she set classes and had an interpreter run the lessons. The children were learning to speak English and French as well as reading and writing. During that time, Emmy had seen two of the children adopted by loving families in the USA.

Now, in the middle of November 1974, Micky was back in her life, and her family was whole.

On a warm autumn day, the wet season now coming to an end, making the temperature more comfortable and the days shorter, Emmy and Mia walked along Nguyen Trai. Cars and motorbikes drove by, though Emmy had become accustomed to the traffic and noise. She still hadn't grown used to the crush of people though, and doubted she ever would – she never had in London.

Mia was practising her Vietnamese on Emmy. Like many children, it had been easier for her to pick up another language.

'Thank you. Cảm ơn bạn.'

'Thank you. Cảm ơn bạn.'

'Your turn, Mummy,' Mia said.

Emmy tried. 'Come on bun.'

'Mine,' Mia said. 'Tôi.'

They came to a halt. On the step leading into the orphanage sat a child: a little boy with light brown hair and light skin, greenish-blue eyes. *Not Vietnamese enough,* Emmy noted. The boy looked a little older than Mia, although he would not be taller than her.

'Hello,' Emmy said.

The little boy looked at her, his eyes full of tears.

'Mama,' he said and pointed down the road.

Emmy saw a woman standing at the corner looking at her and the little boy. Then she hurried away.

'Stay here, Mia,' Emmy said and sat Mia on the step beside the little boy.

She rushed down the street, glancing back at Mia on the step, pushing people out of her way. When she reached the corner, there was no sight of the woman. The street branched into several alleyways, and Emmy simply couldn't tell where the woman had gone. She could not leave Mia on the step alone, so hurried back.

'He's hungry, Mummy,' Mia said. She had opened her lunch box – Emmy always took lunch for her and Mia – like the other westerners, she never ate food the orphans could have. The little boy was eating the baguet Mia had given him.

'His name is Leo,' Mia told her.

'Leo,' Emmy said. The little boy looked at her and gave her an envelope in his hand.

Emmy took it and said, 'Let's go inside.'

'Mama,' Leo said.

'I'm sorry,' Emmy said. 'Help Leo, Mia.'

Mia took the boy's hand while Emmy picked up the bundle of possessions that sat on the step next to him. Upstairs in the sitting room, he sat on the floor with Mia, while Emmy made him food and drink. He was quiet, staring at the wall.

Mary-Anne and Emmy sat at the staff kitchen table reading the letter Leo had held up to her. It was well written in English and must have been the work of a letter writer.

Dear Australian Ladies, it said.

Please look after my boy. His father is an Australian

soldier.

I thought he loved me, he told me he loved me, he told me his name was Harry Johnson, that he would write to me. I did not know that I was pregnant. He went back to Aussie in January 1967. He said he lived in a town called Port Augusta. He did not write to me like he said he would.

I cannot look after my boy now; my family has arranged for me to marry a man far away from our village near the city of Ba Ria to hide their shame. This man will only take me. He will not take my son, another man son.

Please look after my Leo for me, always tell him I love him. I don't know what else to do, my father will not spend any more money feeding us if I do not accept this marriage.

I hope for Leo a better life, if there is a place where he will be loved and cared for. If not please look after him until he is old enough to look after himself.

I have bought much shame on my family; I must do what they have arranged for me.

The letter was signed *Chau.*

Emmy could not stop the tears running down her face. She wiped her cheeks with the back of her hand.

On Wednesday, 27th November, Emmy had an appointment with Geoffrey Price, the Australian Ambassador in Saigon. She sat opposite him, a large Jarrah desk between them, a picture of Elizabeth II, the Queen of England on the wall behind him – no picture of Gough Whitlam, the Prime Minister of Australia, anywhere.

Emmy had spent her waiting time reading *The West Australian* newspaper; it was a week out of date. The air-conditioning was a blessing – nowhere in Saigon had she been in air-conditioned premises.

'What can I help you with, Miss Cannon?' the Ambassador asked.

Emmy told him: she had renewed her and Mia's passports in London but needed to update Mia's birth certificate. She told him she had tried to do this with a staff member but they had been unhelpful, so she had insisted on speaking to him.

'I understand this is not something you would deal with yourself, but I am not getting any help from your staff,' Emmy said. 'I would like my daughter to have her father's name included on her birth certificate. I didn't think this would be a problem.'

'Unfortunately, these matters can be quite complicated, Miss Cannon,' he said.

The Ambassador looked at her from across the desk. Emmy couldn't tell if he was angry or tired.

'What are you doing in Saigon?' he asked.

'I'm teaching at the Sacred Heart Orphanage.'

'With Mary-Anne Robertson?'

'Yes.'

'Does your child's father know you want to do this?'

'Of course.' Emmy needed to ask for something else, so she swallowed her anger and said, 'We are to be married.'

'Mmm, I see.'

Emmy wanted to shout, 'You don't see! How could you see? You don't know us!' but she didn't; she sat watching him think.

'Is the father in Australia?'

'No. He is a Guard at the American Embassy.'

'He's not Australian.'

Emmy shook her head.

'That could make things more difficult.'

It shouldn't be hard. Micky is Mia's father. Micky had told her it wasn't important; he knew who he was and who Mia was, but

Emmy wanted it to be right.

'I will get one of my aides to look into the necessary documents you will need and get back to you.'

'Thank you.' But Emmy needed to ask one more thing. She paused, knowing what she was going to ask was wrong. but she asked anyway. 'May I ask one more thing?'

The Ambassador was tired; she could see that now.

'Yes.'

Emmy swallowed and said, 'I have a young boy, an orphan, abandoned last week. His father was in the Australian forces. He went back to Australia in January 1967. His name is Harry Johnson. Could you help me find him?'

He looked across the table and said, 'You already know the answer to that question.'

Emmy did know the answer to that question, which was why she had asked it. Then she asked, 'Could I have access to the Australian phone books.'

'I won't say no to that.'

He pushed the button on the intercom on his desk and said, 'Please wait outside, Miss Cannon.'

Chapter Thirty-one

Micky

Micky's palms were sweating. His heart raced, and his stomach turned over. None of it made sense. He pulled the collar of his formal white uniform away from his neck, took a deep breath and calmed himself. William leaned over his shoulder and whispered in his ear. Micky turned his head.

Emmy held his father's arm as she came down the aisle. Mia, dressed in a white satin and lace flower girl dress and carrying a small posy of frangipanis, skipped along in front of them.

Emmy wore a long ivory brocade dress with small sleeves on her shoulders, all covered in embossed flowers. Bands of cream ribbon ran around the scooped neckline and under the bust, and a small ivory lace veil with pearls running around the edges covered her face. His grandmother's veil, posted from the US the day he'd told his mother he had asked Emmy to marry him. It was the veil his mother wore the day she married his father; his sisters had also worn it on their wedding days. Emmy kept the veil in place with a headband covered in pearls. She also carried a posy of frangipani.

William had whispered how beautiful Emmy and Mia were and what a lucky man he was. And he was right. They took his breath away.

William played Otis Redding's _These Arms of Mine_ on his cassette player as Micky's bride came toward him.

The chapel was interdenominational – a normal 'nothing fancy' base chapel, with wooden pews, an altar at the front with a crucifix hanging over it. The Chaplin, although a Catholic priest, agreed to marry them with no religious service.

Micky had said, 'We can wait until I have leave. We can go home to Australia for our wedding. We can invite all the family.'

But Emmy had said, 'No, Micky. We've waited too long, been apart too long. I want to marry you. I don't need a big wedding.'

Indeed, they had waited too long.

Now the Chaplin asked, 'Who gives this woman to be married?'

Michael Brannigan said, 'I do,' and put Emmy's hand in Micky's. He took her flowers and sat in the pew with Kate and Mia.

Micky pushed the veil back from Emmy's face. Her hazel eyes merged into his. The Chaplin asked if there was anyone present who objected to this wedding. Then he said to Micky, 'Repeat after me. I, Michael Francis Brannigan, take you, Emmaline Marie Cannon, be my wedded wife, to have and to hold from this day forward, for better, for worse, for richer, for poorer, in sickness and in health, to love and to cherish, for the rest of my life.'

He then asked Emmy to say the same.

When the Chaplin asked for the rings, William gave them to Micky. Micky took Emmy's hand and placed the ring on her finger as he said, 'This ring is my promise to stay with you forever, my promise to honour you with my body and to share my life with you.'

His eyes were damp as Emmy repeated the promises he had made and placed a gold band on his finger.

The Chaplin then pronounced them 'husband and wife', and announced that he could kiss his bride. Micky took Emmy's face in his hands as she put her hands to his cheeks. He tasted tears as their lips met.

The chapel erupted with cheering and clapping, which

shouldn't have happened – they had planned a quiet wedding – only his parents, Mia, and William, who was in Saigon while the Jackson was in port for shore leave. But there was a crowd in the chapel. The crew of the Jackson, those not on duty, had come ashore. His detachment from the embassy and the girls Emmy worked with at Sacred Heart Orphanage were there. It seemed like every person he knew in Vietnam was in the chapel. When he put his arm around Emmy, Mia ran into his embrace, and he picked her up as William played Mendelssohn's Wedding March on the cassette player. He waltzed down the aisle with his family.

On Christmas Eve morning, after the wedding service and all the necessary legal documents had been signed, William joined them. They shared lunch at his parents' rented outer suburbs apartment in an old French Colonial building surrounded by trees and parks.

Hien and Nguyet, the married couple employed by the apartment owner to 'keep house' as part of the rental agreement, served lunch. Micky had changed out of his uniform, and Emmy wore a sleeveless floral dress that buttoned down the front. Mia had wanted to stay in her flower girl dress.

Michael Brannigan, out of uniform, read telegrams.

> *Darling girl.*
>
> *We are so happy for you and Micky. We are with you in our hearts. Love always.*
>
> *Jacob and Peter.*
>
> *Dear Micky*
>
> *We love and cherish you and welcome Emmaline and Mia into our family.*
>
> *Happiness always,*
>
> *Karen and Jessie.*

Cake and coffee were being served when the phone rang. Kate pushed her chair back.

'Kate!' Michael said.

Kate retained her seat. 'Your mother has never gotten used to having people working for her,' Michael said.

Micky could see the love in his father's eyes as he made the comment. The same often happened at home, his mother not liking having a housekeeper and driver. Meg and Benjamin had come with the house when his grandmother had died. His mother could drive and was happy to do her own housekeeping, but the house in San Francisco was too big and the gardens too large for her to manage on her own. Benjamin drove, with her as a guide, and Meg pottered around the house with her until his mother insisted they retire and live as part of the family in their last years. She reluctantly hired new staff.

'A phone call for Miss Emmy,' Hien said as he bought the phone to the table.

Micky saw a sparkle in his father's eyes.

'Hello?' Emmy said. Then her eyes filled with tears. 'Papa, Papa. Yes, I am.' Micky could only hear Emmy's side of the conversation. 'Mama, yes, yes. I love you too. Mia come and talk to Oma and Opa. Joey, I miss you too, and Jimmy. Happy Christmas. Papa, I don't know. When Micky has leave. I love you. See you soon. Goodbye.'

Emmy handed the phone back to Hien and wiped her eyes. 'Thank you,' she said to Michael.

Emmaline

Emmy wiped her tears away – it was her wedding day, she would not cry. She did, however, miss her parents and brothers, and she could have waited until Micky could arrange leave to go home for her wedding. But she wanted to marry Micky – that was more important than any wedding party she could have. She had Micky and Mia, and that was what mattered most.

After lunch, they left Mia with her grandparents and spent the day together, walking along the riverbank and sitting in the shade. They had two days to share.

Micky said, 'I'm pretty sure the extra day I won in the Christmas ballot was rigged, but I wasn't going to say no.'

He'd booked a suite in the Continental Hotel, and they made love in that room.

Emmy stood in front of Micky and undid the buttons on his checked shirt; opened the zip on his jeans. She would never get used to the scars on his chest, knowing how they'd been inflicted. He always lowered his head when she saw them, but not today; he held himself up straight, looked into her eyes and unbuttoned her dress. The dress fell to the floor. He knew where the clasp on her bra was now and opened it. He bent his head; caressed her breasts with his mouth. She could never hold herself upright when he did that and leant into him.

Emmy threw her arms around his neck and sought his mouth, then they were naked in the bed, and he was stroking her neck, running his fingers through her hair, around her body, arousing her body.

Her body reacted, aching, wanting. She caressed and kissed Micky's neck, his chest, his thighs, her mouth exploring his body, enjoying his body. And she made love with him.

Micky

Micky remembered the first time he'd made love with Emmy. How shy she'd been, how his tears had wet her hair, how innocent she'd been; how innocent *he'd* been. Emmy made love with him, challenging his doubts about his physical and mental scars.

He had champagne delivered to the room, and this time the

chocolate-covered strawberries were chocolate-covered strawberries. Ceiling fans moved the hot air around their sweat-covered bodies. They slept in each other's arms.

The sunset dinner was eaten in the room before sharing a shower. Then they wandered the streets of Saigon hand in hand. Even in the dark, the air was warm, the traffic frantic, and people rushed around. Night rain trickled on their faces.

Midnight mass was celebrated at the Notre Dame Cathedral where they met his parents and took Mia back to the hotel room with them. The concierge at the Continental Hotel was surprised when Micky had asked him to provide a bed for Mia. But he had been without his family for too long and wanted them close to him when he could have that comfort.

When he was on duty, he would sleep in the billets at Marine House. But that wasn't tonight. Tonight he slept with his family. He had shared a room at his parents' apartment with Emmy once or twice over the past few weeks when his parents had taken Mia out. They had never shared Emmy's room at her apartment — that would have been disrespectful to Mary-Anne. It would be different now they were married.

Micky woke to find Emmy sitting beside him. Moonlight reflected in the tears on her face as her hand hovered over the scars on his back. He turned over and pulled her into his arms. 'Hey, hey, I'm okay. I'm safe. I'm here with you,' he said.

Emmy curled into his body, and he held her until she stopped trembling, until her tears stopped wetting his chest, until she fell asleep.

He closed his eyes and slept.

The next time Micky opened his eyes, his daughter stood beside the bed, looking into them. How she'd done that without him waking was a surprise. Light from the sunrise came in the windows.

'I need a wee,' she said.

He put his finger up to his lip and whispered, 'Shush, don't wake Mummy.' He moved Emmy off his stiff arm, but she stirred and said, 'What's wrong?'

'Nothing. Go back to sleep.' He moved her away and pulled the sheet around her shoulders. Luckily, he had shorts on and swung his legs out of bed.

Mia's eyes widened when she saw the scars on his chest; he grabbed his t-shirt from the floor and pulled it over his head.

'Does it hurt?' Mia asked, reaching toward him.

'Not anymore.'

'Who did that to you?'

What could he tell her? She had already seen enough of war. His heart raced as he remembered when Emmy had told him about the Kibbutz. He wouldn't lie to her, so said, 'Someone who didn't like me very much?'

'Why, Daddy?'

'I don't know, Mia.' And he didn't. He had been in Vietnam to look after the sick and wounded, and he had done that for both sides. 'It was a long time ago, and they can't hurt me anymore.'

She put her arms around his neck, and he lifted her onto his knee. 'I love you, Daddy,' she said.

'And I love you, Mia,' he told her.

Then he knew he had a right to exist, a right to be alive. Everything he had done to stay alive had meaning.

Mia whispered in his ear, 'Wee, wee, Daddy.'

Emmaline

Emmy woke to the sound of the door opening and Mia chatting away.

'Daddy and me made your breakfast,' she said as a trolley pushed by a hotel employee came into the room.

Emmy stretched her arms above her head and locked eyes

with Micky. *Something has changed. What?* He leaned over her, and she wrapped her arms around his neck, kissed his lips. Her body longed for his, but their daughter was standing beside the bed. Mia jumped onto it, and Emmy snuggled into her, kissing the top of her head.

Mary-Anne and the girls had bought her pink silk pyjamas. They had laughed about how much time she would have them on. Sharing their room with Mia meant a lot more than she had expected.

'Yummy,' Emmy said. 'What time is it?'

'7.30.' Micky said.

He set the trolley up next to the table in the window. It had fruit and pastries, a bowl of rice bubbles, milk in a jug and coffee in a pot, toast and bacon and eggs. *Too much food for three people.*

The sun had risen, bringing the heat with it, but the ceiling fans kept the room cool. Micky set out three places, and Emmy sat opposite him with Mia on her right.

'It's Christmas day,' he said. 'I have gifts for you.'

Micky walked around the table and dropped to one knee in front of her, a little felt box in his hand. He opened it, held it out to her.

'You didn't have to,' Emmy said. Indeed, he didn't have to do that, but he had. Her hand trembled when he held it, and she fought back the tears.

'I know,' he said. 'I wanted to.'

He put the ring on her finger; it matched her wedding ring and had one diamond sitting on the band. He said to Mia, 'I have something for you too. Put out your hand, and close your eyes.'

Mia did as told.

Micky sat on the chair and opened another felt box: placed a solid silver bracelet on her wrist, the catch closed with a bluebird. 'Open your eyes.'

Mia stared at the bracelet. She'd never had anything like it before. Emmy was sure the bracelet wasn't silver, even though it looked. She knew Micky would give his daughter gold but she was too young for yellow gold; he would have given her white gold, which looked like silver.

'Thank you, Daddy. We have a present for you too,' Mia said. She left the table, hunted around in the case, and pulled out a package, which she handed to Micky. It was a picture of her and Emmy etched into a medallion, hanging on a silver chain.

His fingers were clumsy as he put the chain around his neck so Emmy stood and closed the clasp for him. His eyes looked into hers. Something was different. The sadness she saw when he didn't think she was looking; the memories he hid from her, pushed back, seemed not to be stalking him so closely, giving him space.

He said, 'I love you. I love you both.'

Christmas day 1974: the excitement at the Sacred Heart Orphanage filled everyone. Father Bob, the Embassy Chaplin, had agreed to play Santa for the children, and over the past six weeks, the staff had been gathering gifts. Emmy had told Mia Father Christmas would be bringing her a gift when he came to see all the children.

Food had been stored. Meat and chicken had always been expensive and had become scarce over the past month. After Communist forces had launched an attack to the north of Saigon early in December, supplies from some country areas were no longer available. A celebration banner declaring 'Welcome Mr and Mrs Brannigan' hung on the wall in full view of Micky and Emmy when they arrived at the orphanage. Now they were busy setting tables and laying out food.

Then came a knock on the door, then a pounding on the door. The children ran down the stairs to be greeted by Father Christmas. They ran behind him as he came up the stairs into the living room, where stood the Christmas tree. He plopped himself on an allocated chair and began searching through his bag. Calling out names, he handed out gifts, talked to the children, wished them well, told them stories about his reindeer. He drank a glass of milk and took a bag of carrots for his reindeer when he left.

Then came another knock on the door. No more visitors were expected, and Emmy frowned as she answered the door.

At the orphanage door stood William, and sailors from the Jackson, as well as two US Marines and Michael and Kate, their arms ladened. Emmy couldn't express her gratitude in words. The extra food was carried upstairs and laid out on the table.

Emmy stood wrapped in Micky's arms, watching the food disappear. Mia sat with Leo: they'd become friends over the past weeks.

Michael and Kate rolled up their sleeves and helped the children. The marines and sailors stood awkwardly watching. Children who would never know their fathers, whose features showed their mixed race, who couldn't be hidden in the population.

William spoke to one of the boys, Jack. He was ten years old, his black hair tightly curled, his skin too dark to be Vietnamese, his features not Vietnamese enough.

'What happens to the children?' he asked Emmy.

Emmy tried not to let her emotions overtake her: she still struggled when talking about the children. Her memories, memories of a decision she'd almost made, were too close sometimes. She pulled herself together and said, 'We hope we can find the children families. Mary-Anne works hard at that. I would like …' Emmy knew how fortunate she'd been.

Micky squeezed her shoulder, and she looked into his eyes. He knew. She leant into him and held his arms around her.

When the food was devoured, the children spent time playing

with their new toys, the younger ones soon fell asleep in the nursery. In the back garden, under a humid blue sky, a game was set up. Emmy had played softball at school, and this game looked similar. The older children were throwing and catching with the gloves and balls they'd received. William threw a ball with Jack.

Emmy and Kate stood at the kitchen sink overlooking the courtyard, Mary-Anne having sent all the local staff home to their families. Two of them had taken the 'grandmothers' home. There was a lot of cleaning to do.

Michael had offered to help in the kitchen, but Kate had sent him outside. Emmy watched Micky in the backyard trying, without much success, to arrange children into teams. He was laughing and smiling, sharing time with his father and his friends. She twisted the rings on her finger.

'I thought I would have to live without him,' Emmy said.

Kate put an arm around her and said, 'He is alive because he loves you.'

Emmy nodded. Alive because he loved her, suffered so much because he loved her.

Chapter Thirty-two

Micky

Michael Brannigan had been in Saigon since early September 1974 as part of a diplomatic mission sent to Saigon by the US Congress. Michael's experience in the Navy, his forty years of service, made him ideal for assessing the situation. Congress would no longer approve funds to support the South Vietnamese government without advice.

Michael told Micky in the middle of February: 'Ambassador Martin hopes Saigon will not suffer an invasion by the communist forces; that the South Vietnamese government will survive. I cannot see that happening without a huge increase in aid from us. I will not recommend more American troops be sent to Vietnam; I cannot agree to more American lives being lost in Vietnam.'

'I will be sending Kate home soon. You should do the same with Emmy and Mia.'

Micky tried, but Emmy's determination had surprised him. They argued over it – he hadn't thought that possible.

Emmy sat opposite him at the kitchen table in her apartment, Mia on the floor colouring pieces of paper near her feet. Mary-Anne was out, so he bought up the subject again.

'You will have to leave soon, Emmy.'

'I know, Micky, but not yet. Please, not yet ... you said we would ...'

'I know.' He poured the coffee.

The liquid spilt when Emmy picked up the cup.

He had promised her, and he understood. He tried again. 'Promise me you will look after Mia.' He knew though Emmy would never let any harm come to Mia.

'You know I will do that,' she said. 'But Leo … I have to find his father. He might have a father who doesn't even know he's alive, who might want him in his life. I have to keep trying. I can't leave him on his own.'

They both looked at Mia sitting on the floor. His daughter, he hadn't known Mia was alive until she was four years old. Emmy looked into his eyes and said, 'I love you, Micky, and I love Mia.'

She flicked her tears away, and he reached across the table and wiped her face. 'Promise me you will go when I tell you it's time to leave. Promise me,' he said.

'I promise,' she said. Her head bowed to hide her tears.

Micky lifted her chin and said, 'And take Leo with you.'

Emmaline

Emmy had spent the last few months trying to contact Leo's father. She'd sent letters to every H. Johnson who lived in Port Augusta, a simple note that said she was looking for a Harry Johnson who had served in Vietnam in 1965-67, asking them to contact her.

She had received one reply: from a lady, Harriette Johnson, who wished her well in her endeavour, saying her grandson, Alexander, had served in Vietnam.

Micky understood how important it was for her to find Leo's father. He also knew she would not let any harm come to Mia. By making her promise to look after Mia, he was making sure she would leave.

Micky could not leave. He had his duty to perform. And Emmy had her duty to him and his daughter, *their* daughter. Emmy had to leave. But she would stay as long as she could.

The next day Emmy received a letter.

Dear Miss Cannon,

My name is Alexander Johnson. My grandmother has informed me that you are trying to trace a soldier named Harry Johnson who served with the Australian forces in Vietnam.

The letter my grandmother received stated that this Harry Johnson left Vietnam in January 1967.

My battalion of the AIF left Vietnam in January 1967. We were stationed at Nui Dat, in the province of Phuoc Tuy, near the city Ba Ria. I am presuming your letter is with regard to a friendship Harry Johnson had with a local girl.

I have included my current address if you wish to contact me.

Yours sincerely,
Alexander Harold Johnson.

Emmy replied,

Dear Mr Johnson,

Thank you for your reply.

Yes, my letter is in regard to a relationship with a local girl.

I am teaching at the Sacred Heart Orphanage in Saigon where a young boy has been left in our care. His mother left him with a note saying his father was a Harry Johnson who left Vietnam in January 1967. I am trying to contact this man to let him know of his son. The mother's letter mentioned the city Ba Ria. Her name is Chua

Two weeks later another letter arrived.

Emmy tucked Mia into bed with her that night and cried herself to sleep. Then she wrote back.

The next letter arrived on the 14ʰ March 1975.

seems to be no peaceful way for this to happen. I questioned what I was doing, who was I helping, who could I trust?

I suppose that is the nature of civil war, brother and sister against each other, fathers and sons on opposite sides.

Please ensure Leo is on the first flight to Australia you can arrange. I have included a telephone number you can contact me on.

Yours sincerely,

Harry.

Chapter Thirty-three

Micky

Towards the end of March, away from central Saigon, on a street lined with trees, it was lunchtime at Kate and Michael's apartment. Micky had a few hours off to spend with his friends and family.

Two little girls sat at a separate small table ladened with colouring pencils, paper and food. One had dark hair and dark eyes, the other had blonde hair and blue eyes. Micky's and Simon's daughters. They'd had an immediate connection when they'd met and had become friends over the past few days.

'We are taking him, Jack, home on Monday. He will be home for Easter,' William said. 'There has been a lot of paperwork and a lot of … I don't like to say bribes – I understand why – but there is no other word I can use.'

It had been a complicated process for William and Becky to adopt Jack, the process starting on Christmas Day when William had first met the boy. Micky had seen the connection William and Jack had made. Becky, of course, would have the final say in such a decision, but Micky knew she would agree.

Becky was a navy brat, like him and Simon. They had met in Elementary school and gone to High school together. One day in Junior High, Simon had announced he was going to marry Becky, and ten years later, he did.

Now Becky was married to William, and she was radiant, her fair skin glowing, her blue eyes sparkling. She and William were expecting a child in August.

'It will all be worth it when we get home.' William said, smiling at Becky.

'Will you be leaving soon, Mrs Brannigan?' William asked Kate.

'Kate, William. Call me Kate. I will be leaving when Michael does.'

The look that passed between his parents told Micky they had argued about this too. It also told him his father had had as much success as he'd had in getting his wife to agree to leave.

'We can take Mia with us if you would like,' William said to Micky.

'No!' Emmy cried, startling everyone at the table. Then she said, 'I'm sorry, excuse me.' She placed her napkin on the table, pushed her chair back and left the room.

Micky followed her out onto the balcony, where she stood leaning on the railing, her shoulders heaving.

'Hey,' he said, turning her around and wrapping her in his arms.

'Don't take Mia away from me,' she mumbled into his chest.

He held her away from him. 'I won't do that. You know I won't do that.' Then he pulled her close again, and she clung to him.

Emmy had lost weight, and her makeup did not hide her tired eyes. He knew the workload at the orphanage had increased now Mary-Anne and Emmy were the only westerners still there. The other girls had evacuated, and the French sisters of Loretto had returned to France. Food was becoming difficult to find, and the black market was the only place to buy many items. It was expensive and required a lot of haggling. He knew how difficult that was for Emmy.

Emmy was arranging visas and documents for Leo and the other children, which also required a lot of haggling, but she had made a commitment to Leo to reunite him with his father. Micky understood why she did this: Mia could have been Leo, abandoned by a father who didn't know she was alive. He shuddered when he thought of that.

'I won't do that,' he repeated.

Emmaline

Emmy curled into Micky's embrace, her head resting on his chest. Inside, the ceiling fan kept the air comfortable, but out on the balcony, where there was none, it was hot and humid. Thankfully, the thick smoky air that choked central Saigon didn't surround the apartment.

Emmy felt Micky shudder as he said, 'I won't do that.' She stayed in his arms, breathing in his scent, the fabric of his uniform rough against her skin.

'Can you stay tonight?' she asked.

He shook his head. 'I'm sorry.' His duty was to protect the embassy, and he would sleep in the billets at Marine House.

The door to the balcony opened.

'Okay?' Kate asked.

'Yes.' Emmy wiped her eyes then pushed Micky away. 'I'm okay. Go in. I'll be in in a minute.'

Emmy saw Micky's eyes meet his mother's. He released his embrace and kissed her cheek before opening the glass doors and disappearing inside. She ran a finger through her hair; wiped her cheeks again; stood looking down the tree-lined street, across the grass and tree-covered parkland, at the old French colonial buildings. A pink and blue painted pagoda was visible through the treetops.

'It is beautiful,' she said.

'Yes,' Kate answered. 'But only for some.'

That's true. Emmy had seen so much poverty, so many hungry children. 'Would it be any better under the communists?'

'I don't know.' Kate looked over the balcony, her eyes distant, looking into the past. 'Some people hope that will happen. It usually doesn't.'

'I'm sorry I messed up lunch.'

'Don't be silly. William understands.'

She put her arm around Emmy and said, 'There's plenty of food here. Mia won't go hungry.'

Emmy nodded. She remembered being hungry and cold. She would not let that happen to Mia.

'And we will do what we can to help the other children,' Kate said. 'You have to eat. You can't look after Mia if you don't look after yourself.'

'I know. But I'm not very hungry today.' She had pushed her meal around her plate, hoping no one would notice. But Micky and Kate had.

Then Kate said, 'You understand that I can choose to stay with Michael.' Emmy nodded. 'And you know that you cannot choose to stay with Micky, don't you?' Kate said.

'Yes.' Emmy indeed understood: she had to keep Mia safe. That was something she could do.

Chapter Thirty-four

Emmaline

The following Wednesday, Emmy had an appointment at the Australian Embassy in Caravelle House. She sat reading old magazine stories of the cyclone that had destroyed Darwin on Christmas Eve, surprised by what she didn't know. She was thankful she had no friends or family in that part of Australia.

Emmy expected to get a new copy of Mia's birth certificate showing Micky as her father.

'I'm sorry, Miss Cannon.'

Emmy was in the office with a minor member of the embassy staff. Phillip Jones, the nameplate on the desk read.

'Sorry?' *A simple request*, Emmy thought.

'I haven't received your daughter's amended birth certificate. I have to make further enquiries regarding your request.'

'What?' Emmy said, trying not to be rude.

Michael Brannigan had arranged her new passport: her USA passport as Micky's wife. He couldn't arrange Mia's passport until her birth certificate came back. Before she could have a USA passport, if his name was not on her birth certificate, Micky would have to adopt Mia.

'You understand that by adding your daughter's father's name to her birth certificate, you are giving him rights as her father – rights to make decisions that could conflict with what you want?'

'That will not happen.'

'Can you be sure, Miss Cannon?'

'Mrs Brannigan! I am Mrs Brannigan! We married in

December.'

'Ahh.'

Emmy pulled her anger back. This person was only doing what they had to. She was tired and her stomach was churning. 'Would it help if you had a copy of our wedding certificate?'

'That might.'

Emmy breathed deeply, trying to calm herself and her stomach. She was hot and her eyes weren't focusing. 'I ...'

The next thing Emmy knew was she was lying on a couch, a cold compress on the back of her neck, a wet flannel cooling her face. She opened her eyes.

'What ...?'

'Are you alright?' Several people stood around her.

Phillip Jones said, 'Shall I call a doctor?'

'No, I'm okay,' Emmy said.

She sat up and took the cold, ice-filled glass of water offered Her stomach calmed.

'I will arrange for an embassy car to take you back to Sacred Heart Orphanage,' Geoffrey Price said as he joined the gathered crowd. 'Everyone, back to work now.'

'Thank you,' Emmy said.

The Ambassador sat on the couch beside her. 'I am sending information out to all Australian citizens. It is time to think about leaving Saigon. If the situation deteriorates, I cannot guarantee we will be able to help you leave. You must go while flights are still leaving Tan Son Nhut airport.'

'Yes,' Emmy replied.

She knew when she would leave.

That night, Emmy pulled her knickers up and her skirt down before she swung her legs over the side of the bed. She'd been lying looking at the crucifix hanging on the wall in Mary-Anne's room. Mia was in the front room watching television.

'Yes,' Mary-Anne said. 'You are about twelve weeks pregnant.' She pulled off the surgical gloves and put them in the bin.

'Oh,' Emmy said. Being pregnant explained her unsettled stomach, her disinterest in food. She'd expected what was happening.

'You are happy?'

'Yes.'

'What's this then?' Mary-Anne asked as she wiped Emmy's tears away.

Emmy remembered having Mia … the pain and the fear but more than anything, she remembered being alone. She'd been alone last time she'd been pregnant.

'You will have Micky this time,' Mary-Anne said and sat on the bed beside Emmy.

'Yes.' Micky would be with her this time; she wouldn't be alone. She pushed the doubts away.

She was pregnant. *Micky's baby, my baby.* 'I'm pregnant?' she said, smiling.

'Yes,' Mary-Anne said. 'And you won't be alone.' She pulled Emmy close and held her tight.

Chapter Thirty-five

Emmaline

March the 28th was Good Friday. It had always been a long boring day of church activities when Emmy was young. But today was busy. She had no time to attend church services if she'd wanted to. The school was closed, and Emmy became busy helping Mary-Anne with documents and identification details for their children so they could be ready if an evacuation flight happened.

Sacred Heart Orphanage was one of about 130 orphanages in South Vietnam, and Mary-Anne had friends and colleagues in many. A flood of rumours had been circulating about a flight from Danang and the lengths people had been going to get aboard. This caused much talk about flights leaving Saigon early next week to take the children out of the city.

The Australian Embassy had informed Mary-Anne that the Royal Australian Airforce was bringing relief supplies to refugee camps, and the empty planes might be used to transport children who had approved parents in Australia to Bangkok, to be airlifted by Qantas back to Australia.

Leo had his passport. All Emmy needed for him was his exit visa and a place on a plane out of Saigon. He had a father waiting for him.

Saigon had changed.

The fragile peace accord had been broken almost as soon as it was signed in 1973, but Saigon had remained safe. Now the war was getting closer. Villages to the north were under attack.

There was still hope Saigon would not be overrun for the city was full of refugees, the streets crowded. Broken down and abandoned cars littered the roads. Fires were left burning. A night curfew was in place. Emmy was sure she could hear explosions in the distance. She lied to Mia and told her it was thunder. The peace that had been in place when she had arrived in Saigon was now ebbing away.

Easter Saturday: the children boiled and painted eggs. Micky called and ran around the orphanage, hiding coloured eggs with Emmy and the two Sisters while the rest of the staff kept the children busy. She would tell him their news tomorrow when he had the afternoon off, and Kate and Michael had been less than subtle when they offered to take Mia out.

On Easter Sunday, Emmy and Micky spent the afternoon together. Michael had sent a car for her and Mia, saying he did not want them walking or catching cyclols around the city.

Emmy had news for Micky she wanted him to know. Why she hesitated to tell him, she did not know. He would be happy.

They were alone in the apartment, the ceiling fans whirring in the bedroom keeping them comfortable. His brown eyes searched hers.

'What?' he asked.

He was half-dressed, as she was. She wanted him so much, her body longing for the closeness only making love could give her. Why did she hesitate? What was she afraid of? He loved her; she loved him. Nothing could change that.

'I have news.'

'Leo's visa has come through?' he said.

'No, not that.'

'What?' He could not hide his concern. 'What's wrong, Emmy?'

'Nothing, I'm….' She took his hand and placed it on her belly. '… pregnant,' she murmured.

'Really?'

She nodded.

He smiled. *His smile. The smile he had lost.* Happiness reached all the way to his eyes as they locked with hers. He took her face in his hands, and his body trembled. 'Oh my darling,' he whispered.

Emmy curled into his chest. She wouldn't be alone. She should have known, trusted his love for her.

Micky

Emmy curled into his chest: she was pregnant, having his baby. He wouldn't let her do that on her own again … but she couldn't stay with him either. He was going to have to arrange her passage out of Saigon! That had now just become more urgent. *Leo's visa must come through. I have to get Emmy and Mia out. She doesn't understand the seriousness of the situation.* He could see what could happen, even if his father hadn't told him.

'When?' he asked her.

'September or October. Mary-Anne couldn't give an exact date.'

'Mary-Anne?'

Emmy smiled at him. 'Mary-Anne's a midwife. She was there when Mia was born.'

'I'll be there this time,' he promised.

'Yes.' Emmy said.

She took his face in her hands and kissed his mouth before pulling his body close and holding him tight. Exploring his chest, she ran her fingers down to his shorts. He pulled away.

'Is it safe? Could I hurt you?' He frowned. A silly question? He should know the answer. Was it safe for Emmy, for their baby?

'You will not hurt me, Micky,' Emmy said. The gravity in her voice could not hide her delight or desire.

The joy and happiness of her news surrounded him, a physical presence, something he could touch and hold. He knew he had a right to live, to be alive; he'd discovered that on Christmas day. But the secrets, the memories, the things he'd done to stay alive were still in his mind. He kept them hidden from Emmy, from himself.

He would not let those memories rule his life, so he embraced the joy and happiness, pulling it around him like a blanket. He let it surround him, let it fill his body and soul. He would confront the horrors of those years; he would defeat them, and he would survive them, for Emmy and their children, and for himself.

He made love with her.

Chapter Thirty-six

Emmaline

On Thursday 3rd of April, the Australian Embassy advised Mary-Anne a flight for children with adoptive parents in Australia would be leaving Saigon on the 4th of April.

'One day!' Mary-Anne said. 'How can we be ready in one day!' Emmy shrugged.

They sat together at the staff kitchen table, a table covered in documents, papers and empty or cold tea and coffee cups.

'Leo's visa hasn't come through,' Emmy said.

She had tried every option; she had even offered cash. Harry Johnson's money sent for Leo had given her some bargaining power. She had arranged his passport and had applied for his exit visa when, for some unknown reason, the South Vietnamese government put a hold on exit visas.

No matter how frantic her phone calls had been, she had nothing else she could offer to hurry up the process. She would not use the money she had in place for Mia. She had to draw a line somewhere, and that was it.

But Emmy had Kate and Michael. Michael had used his contacts in the government, but it was easy to lose one little boy in all that was going on. She would not take any money from them.

Emmy had accepted Micky's offer of financial help, but she could see she was not getting anywhere any faster. She would have to wait until the government of South Vietnam agreed to issue Leo with his Exit Visa.

The desperate requests for transport out of Saigon for the bureaucrats' children Emmy dealt with overwhelmed her. She understood: the speculation going around about the vengeance the North Vietnamese army would inflict on those found to have collaborated with the Americans was terrifying. But there was nothing Emmy could do for children who were not at the Sacred Heart Orphanage.

'We can place some of the children on a flight to the US as well. We have two days to do that,' Mary-Anne said.

Emmy rubbed her tired eyes. After a morning of throwing up, her stomach was finally settling down.

They had thirty children ready to evacuate, twenty to the US, ten to Australia. The other twenty children had nowhere to go. No matter how much it was discussed at so-called staff meetings, there was only one solution: the Sisters of Loretto had run the orphanage before Mary-Anne arrived, supported by the local Catholic church. Mary-Anne had told Emmy how horrified she'd been when she arrived at the orphanage; how the care given to the children had been more about their heavenly reward rather than giving them a fulfilling life. When she'd taken on the position as administrator, she'd dismissed, not without objections from the church, several of the sisters; put in place sisters and local staff who would follow her ideals.

'I'd already seen enough of the harm done by entrenched ideas.' She'd patted Emmy on the hand, and Emmy knew how much she had given her. Emmy knew Mary-Anne was the sister Kate and Michael had met.

'Holt International Adoption Agency has chartered a Pan Am aircraft to fly to the US on Saturday. We have been offered places for our children who have adoptive parents waiting for them. Holt has also been able to arrange escorts for the children.' Mary-Anne said.

Their children were older. They did not need looking after as much as the very young. They might even be able to help with the younger children, but they *were* still children, none of them over ten. It would be a long and frightening flight for most of them.

'What about the children going to Australia?' Emmy asked.

'Are you ready to go home?' Mary-Anne asked her.

'No, not yet, *please.*'

'You will have to leave soon.'

'I know.'

'No one knows how much longer Saigon will be safe. Things could change quickly. That is why we are moving the children. It will not be safe for you and Mia, especially if it becomes known her father is a Marine.'

'Wouldn't that protect her?'

'Oh, Emmy,' Mary-Anne said. She patted Emmy's hand like she was a child, and perhaps Emmy *was* thinking like a child. She'd certainly been naïve in her protests against the Vietnam War. Harry Johnson's letter had shown her what civil war meant. She had been young and idealistic. She didn't believe in war. Emmy had always hoped for a world where children could grow up in peace. That seemed far away in Vietnam.

Emmy had heard the rumours of an impending bloodbath. Surely that wasn't true. Surely no one would harm a child because of who her father was. But she knew what had happened to Micky. She had to keep Mia safe.

But right now, she didn't want to talk about it. She placed her hand protectively over her stomach, turned her head, blinked her eyes and forced her tears away.

Mary-Anne still held her hand.

'Will you be alright to escort the children going to Australia on the bus to the airport tomorrow?' Mary-Anne asked.

'On the bus, yes.'

Emmy sat on a bus, the sweat running down her chest wetting her white blouse. Her black pants stuck to the seat. The bus had been half full when it had arrived at the Sacred Heart Orphanage. The children had clambered onto it, sitting three or four to a seat. Unsure, they clung together, their eyes darting around. Most of them had only been out of the orphanage on organised day trips. To see so many other children together, children they didn't know, children who looked different to them, confused them.

The bus driver was a young US Marine, and there was another Marine, Vincent Garcia, on the bus. Emmy remembered Vincent from Christmas day at the orphanage. He sat in the front seat, a weapon tucked between his knees, and she shuddered on realising what that meant. *A bus full of children … how could they need that?*

Emmy wasn't alone. Sister Monica accompanied her, both carrying water and snacks for the children.

Emmy sat in the second row, behind Vincent, a child on her knee. Binh was her name. Mary-Anne had insisted the children who did not have, or did not know, their names be given Vietnamese names, not European names, as had been the case when she arrived at the orphanage.

Binh was their youngest child, just over two years old. Her hair showed too much red, her skin was too pale, and she had the most unusual eyes. Binh's new family, a Lutheran minister and his wife from Adelaide, were waiting for her. Two other children huddled on the chair with Emmy. Even though it was hot, they clung to each other, and to her.

Sister Monica sat with the remaining children: three in the seat with her and four squashed together behind her. The oldest child being evacuated today was An Dung, an eight-year-old boy.

A few people gathered around the bus. When the driver ensured that everyone was seated, he moved the bus forward, forcing those gathering around it to move aside. The drive through the streets of Saigon showed Emmy what she hadn't seen when she was walking or in a vehicle at ground level. From the bus window, she saw the streets littered with broken-down cars, building after building shuttered closed. Rubbish lay all around, and fires burned unattended. Most startling were the boots, uniforms and even weapons lying abandoned.

Every time the bus stopped, a crowd would gather. Vincent Garcia had moved his weapon onto his knees. The children had become aware of the attention the bus attracted, and some had begun to cry. Emmy held her children close, and Sister Monica, with An Dung's help, calmed the other children.

The bus stopped at its final pickup point, which took longer than it should to ensure all the children and their caregivers were safely aboard. Again, a large crowd had gathered, and people now banged on the windows. Mothers on the street began crying out, pushing their children forward, seeking a place on the bus.

Vincent Garcia rose from his seat; held his rifle within sight. As the bus was about to move, a rock hit the front window, which cracked but did not break. Children screamed, and men clambered up the steps onto the bus, but Vincent used the butt of his rifle to push them back.

Emmy pulled the children on the seat with her close; she could not stop them from crying, but they were not screaming like some of the others behind her. The bus began to rock back and forth.

Vincent stood on the step of the bus, raised his rifle and sent one shot into the air. That startled the crowd, then he lowered his rifle and aimed at those closest to him. They backed away, and the driver moved the bus away as fast as he could.

Emmy comforted her children. Every time the bus stopped at a traffic light, people gathered, and the children cried. But no one tried to board the bus. At the checkpoint into the airport, another crowd had gathered, but they were kept away by the security guards located there.

The bus pulled into the airport, onto the tarmac and parked next to one of two Royal Australian Airforce planes. Vehicles rumbled around refuelling and stocking the planes. Huge metal shapes with men in uniform clambering over them was nothing the children would be familiar with. Noise and dust filled the air, and still the children clung to each other, thirsty and afraid.

Emmy helped the children off the bus and sat them in the shade of the plane's wing, ensuring they all had water. Then she said to Sister Monica, 'Can you mind my children?'

Gulping in air, she stumbled away, her hand on the side of the bus to steady herself. It was quieter, more private, at the back of the bus, and Emmy swayed and leaned her head on the metal.

'You okay, Mrs Brannigan?' Vincent Garcia said, handing her his water canteen.

'I'm …' Emmy guzzled the water down. Her legs felt like jelly. She didn't want to throw up, and her hand was still shaking when she handed Vincent's canteen back to him.

'Yes, thank you.' Then she heard boots running, felt hands take her arms and turn her around. She buried her head in Micky's chest.

Micky

Micky held Emmy tight. She was trembling as she clung to him, disregarding the heat and humidity. He shoved his fears away; held her tighter. She had to leave, it was time for her to leave, but he never wanted to let her go.

'Micky,' Emmy said.

He tried to ease her away, to make sure she wasn't hurt, but her fingers gripped the fabric of his shirt. He ran his fingers through her hair, lifted her chin to look into her eyes.

'I'm okay,' she said and loosened her grip. 'I'm okay. The children?' Emmy asked.

'Okay. They are okay. Sister Monica is with them, and Mary-Anne is here now.'

He could see she wasn't hurt, but he could see how frightened she was, how she tried to hide it from him.

Emmy shielded him, understanding the line he was walking, that he wanted to be more, could be more, more for Emmy.

'I'm here, Emmy. Let me be here,' he said. 'Let me ...'

He wanted to be for her what she was for him; he wanted her to know he could give her what she had given him.

She rested her brow on his chest. 'I can't lose you again, Micky … I can't,' he heard her whisper.

'You won't lose me,' he said. 'I'm here. Let me be here for you.'

'You are always here,' she said. Then she wrapped her arms around him, clung to him, held him. Then she lifted her face to him. 'Micky, why would people want to hurt children?'

He had no answer.

'I have to get back,' she said next. 'I have to help settle the children.'

He led her back to the front of the bus; could feel her holding herself, leaning less on him as they reached the crowd of children and grown-ups milling around the planes.

'I'll see you tonight,' Micky said.

'Tonight.' Emmy smiled, her eyes determined.

He strode away, into the heat and the noise, into the crowd. Plane engines, airport vehicles, military personnel, children crying, adults soothing them. He turned to look back at her, but the dusty air clouded his view; he could barely see where she was. Then he saw Mary-Anne wrap Emmy in her arms and wipe her cheeks.

Emmy had a task to do, and he had his duty to perform. He was covered in sweat, his heart thumping. They would have dinner tonight: him, Emmy and Mia.

Then she would leave. Somehow, he would make it happen.

Emmaline

A good hour passed as Emmy settled all the children on the RAAF plane for the flight to Bangkok. They were young and afraid. The aeroplane was large and noisy, the aircrew unfamiliar. Mary-Anne would sit nearby, with the children sitting in the cargo hold of the huge metal object, strapped down for take-off and landing.

Emmy kissed and cuddled her children. She said goodbye; told them they were going on an exciting journey to a new land where they would always be safe, where there were families waiting to love and care for them.

Then she stood with Mary-Anne at the foot of the cargo ramp. 'I'll be back when the RAAF plane returns. There are a few more documents to get ready for tomorrow's flight, then you should be able to head home,' Mary-Anne said.

Mary-Anne carried Binh, who would sit on her knee for the ninety-minute flight. 'The Red Cross and government officials will look after the children on the Qantas flight from Bangkok to Sydney,' she said.

'Time to go, miss.' The officer at the top of the plane's tailgate called to Mary-Anne.

Emmy snuggled into Binh's face, kissing her cheek and ruffling her hair as she tried not to cry.

She watched the plane taxi away.

More children were being settled into the other RAAF plane, children from other orphanages and Emmy's help was appreciated. As she settled these children, she heard fire engine sirens racing away from the airport.

Chapter Thirty-seven

Emmaline

Six o'clock had come and gone by the time Emmy opened the door to the Sacred Heart Orphanage. The phone was ringing and she wondered why no one was answering it. She hurried into Mary-Anne's office and picked up the phone.

'Yes, yes, I have two mother care nurses I can send to help, straight away, yes,' Emmy said and put the phone down. She rested her hand on the desk, unable to believe the words she had heard.

The Adventist hospital needed help. Emmy wasn't a nurse, couldn't do anything to help at the hospital, but she had staff who could.

'Sister Monica,' she called.

Emmy organised her mothercraft nurses, packing what supplies she had and arranging a taxi. Fifteen minutes later, she stood on the step, watching the taxi drive away.

A plane full of children on its way to America had crashed, the journey to safety ending before it began. None of the children she cared for and loved was on that plane, but her heart still crumpled.

News of the crash had reached the orphanage while Emmy was on her way back. She could see the sadness in the staff as they prepared the evening meal for their children.

She made another phone call, then went about helping to prepare the remaining children's meals and bedtime; she sat with Mia and Leo while they ate and tried not to hold Mia too tight when she said goodbye.

It was late when Emmy made her way back to her apartment, an age seeming to have passed since the bus ride to the airport. Mia was safe, she knew, yet every now and then the tears in her eyes spilled over, and she would brush them away. She had work to do, and it could not wait. Her mother-care nurses had returned from the hospital with grim news.

The remaining children at the Sacred Heart Orphanage were asleep, the grandmothers sleeping with them. Emmy insisted on keeping a light on that night. She had finished the documentation for the children flying to the USA tomorrow and had called a taxi to take her home.

She opened the black door and made her way up the stairs, each one further away than the previous one. Micky slumped on the floor, his back against her apartment door, his camouflage uniform covered in mud. He stared at the top of the staircase. She could not tell if he was asleep or awake, his eyes were open, but he did not seem to see her. Emmy stood in front of him.

'Where's Mia?' he asked as his eyes focused on her.

'She's safe. She's with your parents.'

Emmy slid down the door and sat next to him, took his mud-covered hand in hers.

'They were all dead, Emmy,' he said.

'Not all of them. The pilot saved some. Not all of the children died,' she told him.

'We never found any alive.'

He put his hand on her belly, and she placed her hand over it. She looked into his eyes, then pulled him into her arms. Micky dropped his head on her shoulder, and she held him while he cried.

Micky

Micky had been having a drink with his detachment before

having the night off to spend with Emmy and Mia. He'd heard sirens about four. Soon after, the detachment was called back on duty, told to report to Tan Son Nhut in camouflage. They were told a plane had crashed; they were to search for survivors and were given torches to carry into the night.

The field was strewn with wreckage, plane fuselage smouldering on the green grass. Tiny boots, tiny clothing lay in the mud; papers fluttered in the breeze. Toys were strewn about.

Soldiers from the South Vietnamese army also searched the crash site. He'd heard voices call: a baby found alive. Where he searched with the men of his detachment, none were found alive.

'Come on,' Emmy said. 'Let's go inside.'

He pushed himself up and held her hand as she stood. She was unsteady on her feet, and dark circles sat under her eyes. He steadied her. Taking a deep breath, Emmy put the key in the lock and opened the door.

Emmy guided him to the sofa and went into the kitchen to put the kettle on; made coffee. Then she sat beside him on the couch.

'Can I stay tonight?' he asked.

'Please,' Emmy said. She rested her head on his shoulder, the empty cup slipping from her fingers and falling to the floor.

'Are you okay?' he asked, frowning.

Emmy nodded, but she was asleep. He carried her to the bedroom, turned the fans on high and lay her on the bed. Her short hair stuck out, and he pushed the pieces back in place.

'You have to leave,' he whispered. 'I will always be with you; I will never leave you, but you have to take Mia and go to safety.'

He was filthy, covered in mud, sweat and grime; he couldn't lay beside her like that.

Emmaline

The sound of the front door opening woke Emmy. Micky lay

beside her naked. She was in her underwear, her clothing folded on the bottom of the bed Mia slept in; her shoes were tucked under that bed. She pulled the sheet over Micky, lifted her satin wrap from the hook on the bedroom door, closed it and went into the living room.

Mary-Anne stood in the middle of the room, tears on her face. Emmy wrapped her in her arms.

'Okay?' Emmy asked.

'Yes.'

The clock on the wall told her it was past midnight. The washing machine buzzed, telling her it was finished. She wiped mud from her face and put the kettle on. She desperately needed a shower; she was dirty, her hair dusty and stiff.

Mary-Anne sat at the table and drank the coffee.

'I've finished all the documents for tomorrow,' Emmy said.

'Does anyone know what happened?' Mary-Anne asked.

Emmy shook her head. She pulled Micky's uniform out of the machine and hung it on the airer.

'Not that we know.'

'Will you be ready tomorrow?'

Emmy nodded: it was easier to hide that way. She placed her hand on her stomach. She was okay.

'*No-o-o* …!!' Micky screamed.

Emmy raced to the bedroom, threw open the door. Micky was flailing about in the bed, entangled in the sheet.

'No…' Emmy whispered. She remembered the last time he'd woken in her bed like this.

She sat on the bed, took Micky's shoulders, and held him tight. She could not let him go back there.

'I'm here, Micky, I'm here. You're safe. No one is going hurt you.'

He opened his eyes. 'Emmy!'

'You're safe,' she told him. 'I've got you.'

She wrapped her arms around him and held him until he stopped shuddering; until he stopped remembering; until he fell asleep.

Then she pulled the door shut. She always left a light on when she slept with Micky. The horrors that had happened to him in the dark she could never know.

The living room was empty: Mary-Anne had gone to bed.

Emmy could no longer prevent herself from being sick. She showered and went back to the bedroom; stood beside the bed wrapped in a damp towel, watching Micky sleep. He couldn't go back there; she couldn't let that happen.

She reached out, and Micky opened his eyes.

'Hi,' he said and took her hand.

'I'm here,' she said.

'So am I,' he replied.

Emmy dropped the towel to the floor, climbed into bed, and he pulled the sheet around them.

'I'll always be with you,' he said.

Emmy folded her hands together and rested her head against his chest; she listened to his heart beating. His lips were gentle on hers. He was her husband, and yet they had never shared a bed for a whole night, on their own, not even on their wedding night.

'Goodnight, my darling,' he said and enclosed her in his arms.

Emmy curled into his body and slept.

Chapter Thirty-eight

Emmaline

Emmy woke alone in her bed. She'd obviously slept a few hours: it was nearly six. But the alarm hadn't gone off. Micky's uniform was gone and the airer had been folded back up again. Her stomach objected to the early morning – she tried to ignore it. There was much to do: twenty children were travelling on a Pan-Am plane to the USA today. Then there would be twenty children at the Sacred Heart Orphanage, including Leo and Mia.

After the bus journey yesterday, Mary-Anne decided the orphanage bus would be safer, less conspicuous. This bus could accommodate most of the children and she would arrange a taxi for the others. The orphanage still had its two mothercraft nurses working at the Adventist hospital. Emmy would once again escort the children to the airport.

The journey there was uneventful, but entering the airport was a long and complicated process with all vehicles being searched. The cause of yesterday's plane crash was still unknown, and no Vietnamese could enter the planes.

Again, Emmy cuddled and comforted her children before the plane taxied down the runway and took flight around six in the evening. She would never see those children again. She knew the children from the Sacred Heart Orphanage were as healthy and well-fed as the orphanage could ensure. The children had been in care for longer than many of the other children on the plane, but so many of them had suffered too much in their short lives to ever fully recover.

Emmy spent Saturday evening with Kate and Michael. She cuddled Mia often and spent time talking with Michael.

'Have you seen Micky today?' she asked, glancing at Kate and Mia.

'Not today.'

'He searched the plane crash site,' she told Michael.

He took her hand and said, 'I understand.'

Then he said, 'You will have to leave soon.'

'I know.'

'For Micky's sake, he would not survive if anything happened to you or Mia.'

She would not tell their news without Micky.

'When will you and Kate be leaving?' Emmy asked.

'I will leave with the Ambassador. I hope Kate will leave before then.'

'And Micky?' Emmy said.

'When everyone is gone.'

'His duty?'

'Yes,' Michael said. 'The Ambassador won't order an evacuation. He doesn't want to cause a panic … he still hopes for a peaceful settlement, a settlement that sees South Vietnam survive.'

'Could that happen?'

'Not now,' Michael said. 'This war could have ended in 1969. Peace talks began in 1968, but neither the north nor the south seemed willing. We could have saved many lives, stopped many injuries.' He squeezed Emmy's hand when he said this, then looked over the balcony, down the tree-lined street to the east. Smoke drifted in the sky, the smell of burning carried on the breeze.

'It will end soon. There are many in South Vietnam we fought with – they will have to decide how to protect themselves and their families because North Vietnam will win. I hope we can help those who want to escape and there will be no more bloodshed.'

He patted Emmy's hand and repeated, 'You will have to leave soon.'

On Monday, 7th April: Emmy picked up Mia's birth certificate from the Australian Embassy; too late to get her a US passport, which would take at least four weeks. She would be leaving before then.

'Miss Cannon,' Phillip Jones said. 'The Whitlam government wishes to evacuate more children to Australia.'

Her heart jumped. If only she could get Leo's exit visa.

'Does the Sacred Heart Orphanage have any suitable children?'

'We have three more children with parents in Australia ready to adopt them, and Leo ... his father is waiting for him. I need his exit visa.'

'The government is hoping to get these children out as soon as possible,' Phillip Jones said.

'Will there be transport available?' Emmy had heard last night that the government of South Vietnam had cancelled all evacuation flights for children.

'Yes. The flights will be going ahead.'

When Emmy arrived back at the Sacred Heart Orphanage, the classroom was in chaos, the children taking advantage of the fact she wasn't there. Sister Rose could normally control the situation, but the plane crash on Friday had stripped the heart out of the staff. She popped her head in the door; her daughter and Leo were heavily involved in the mayhem, but she let them be and went to see Mary-Anne.

Her friend looked up from her desk as Emmy opened the door; she picked up a piece of paper and said, 'Leo's visa.'

'Thank God.' Emmy said. 'Have you heard ...?'

'Yes, the Ambassador called. He also insisted that it is time for you and me to consider leaving.'

'What will you do?' Emmy asked.

'We still have children who need looking after. But you will have to leave.'

'I know.'

Chapter Thirty-nine

Micky

The following Saturday, Micky sat holding Emmy's hand while looking out over the Saigon River. The river glowed gold and silver as the sun set, and for a moment, if he didn't look or listen too hard, it was peaceful. Boats spluttered along the water, some driven by engines, others man-powered. People passed by, some slowly, some in a hurry.

Emmy rested her head on his shoulder. The dark circles under her eyes had faded, but she still wasn't eating enough; now he knew why. Morning sickness struck any time of the day.

He had to bring up the topic and said, 'It is time for you and Mia to leave.'

'I know,' Emmy said.

'I can get you a visa as my wife and Mia as my daughter, but Mia only has an Australian passport. It will be easier if you travel to Australia.'

Emmy sucked in her breath; he waited for her reply.

'Australia!' she said.

'Yes.'

'When?' Her hand clutched his.

'I can arrange a place for you and Mia on the next plane evacuating children to Australia.' He lightened his tone. 'The one Leo's going on.'

'Mia would like that.'

He had no doubt Emmy knew that plane would be leaving soon: she had been arranging documents and travel for Leo.

'Micky,' Emmy said, taking his face in her hands and looking into his eyes. Her eyes full of tears, she said, 'That's a good idea. I'm sure Mia and I will be safe with the RAAF. It would be nice to see Mama and Papa too.'

He knew how hard it was for her. He'd promised her he would never leave her, and now he was sending her away. How he wanted this waiting to be over.

Emmaline

Emmy had written to Jacob and Peter telling them her news, wishing she could see the delight she knew the news would bring. She had telephoned her parents – that was difficult. The call had to be booked and a time set, and she was lucky she could use the phone at Kate and Michael's rather than have to go to the post office. Emmy and Mia would fly to Melbourne then onto Perth, where Papa and Mama would meet them at the airport.

The night before she was due to fly home, Emmy and Micky slept with Mia tucked between them. Micky would leave before Emmy needed to be awake, but she sat on the bed, her hands clutching her knees as she watched him dress. When he bent and kissed Mia goodbye, Emmy rose and pulled her robe on, then she put her arms around Micky. At the front door, he said, 'I will see you real soon.' He held her tight and kissed her gently.

'Real soon,' Emmy replied.

She let Micky go. She had to let him go. She leaned her head on the closed door and listened to the echo of Micky's footsteps as he went down the staircase. She heard the black door open and then he was gone.

Emmy had to keep Mia safe and, if she was honest, her unborn child needed more than she could give it in Vietnam. She needed somewhere she felt safe, where she could eat and sit on the sand and watch the waves. She needed somewhere Mia would be safe, and they would all wait for Micky.

The RAAF plane to Bangkok was due to leave mid-afternoon. From there, they would travel to Melbourne onboard a Qantas flight.

Emmy finished packing. She had one bag with a few items of clothing and essentials. She dressed in her blue silk frock, which she wouldn't be able to wear much longer. Mia wore her pink and white striped Petit Bateau dress, which she also wouldn't be able to wear much longer – she'd grown a lot since last summer in Europe.

Emmy left all the clothing she had bought for herself and Mia in Saigon on the bed. Most would be too big and too long, but they could be altered and used. She left all her Vietnamese currency with the clothing. Mary-Anne would forward everything else Emmy wanted to her.

Leo and the children from the orphanage would be in the care of the staff arriving from Australia with the planes. Mary-Anne would drive them to the airport in the orphanage bus, Mary-Anne staying in Saigon.

Emmy closed her case and picked up her backpack, making sure once more all her documents were in place.

'Be good,' she told the child growing within her.

Her stomach rolled, and the walls moved.

'Mummy,' Mia called.

Chapter Forty

Micky

Micky ran as if his life depended on it, because it did. He passed concerned faces as he raced down the hall. His father's footsteps faded as the distance between them increased. He saw his mother standing in a doorway. She put her hands on his chest to stop him and said, 'Walk, Micky. It will frighten her if you run.' She indicated where he should go.

He took a breath, straightened his shirt and somehow walked. When he pulled back the closed curtains, Emmy collapsed into his arms. He looked over her shoulder at the doctor taking his daughter's pulse. He knew that look. That was the look that said: *I've done all I can.*

'She's so hot, Micky. So hot.' Emmy sobbed in his arms. He guided her to a chair beside the bed, and she crumbled onto it. Her sobs faded away as she sat staring at the bed, all the while holding Mia's hand.

They should have been on that plane! It was all arranged. I'd said goodbye. Why weren't they on that plane? It was four in the afternoon … that plane was long gone.

The doctor left the cubical and Micky went to join him. Emmy reached out to stop him.

'I won't be long,' he reassured her.

He shook the doctor's hand as they stood outside the drawn curtains. 'What's wrong?' Micky asked.

'I can't be sure, but I've given her antibiotics in a drip. She could have Meningitis. Her temperature is too high, and we have to get that down.'

Micky looked at the drawn curtains.

'Corporal, you know enough to understand,' Doctor Carlos Perez said as he noted the insignia on Micky's arm badge that told of his rank and occupation. 'The air-conditioning in the hospital will help, and the antibiotics should start to work soon. Her mother?'

'My wife,' Micky said.

'Is she unwell?'

The floor fell out from under Micky; he put his hand out, and the doctor steadied him. 'She's pregnant.'

'Mmm.'

What was happening? Mia was in a hospital bed with tubes in her arm, a mask over her face, her little chest pumping up and down trying to get enough oxygen to survive? And now Emmy?

'What?'

'When is she leaving Saigon?'

'Today.' Micky said. 'She was supposed to leave today.'

'She should rest.'

'Emmy won't leave Mia.'

'No,' the doctor agreed.

Micky saw his parents walking down the ward. He wanted to run like he had when he was a little boy and throw himself into his mother's arms, let her make it all better. But he was a man now.

'I'll see what I can do about another chair.' Dr Perez told him. 'I'll be back soon. You will be staying.'

'Yes.'

Micky stood in a daze until his father caught him by the arm. 'Micky.'

He was too old to be Micky. He should be Mike or Michael, but that was his father's name.

'They don't know, Dad. Maybe Meningitis.'

He heard his mother gulp down her cry. The curtains drawn, he didn't want to talk where Emmy might hear. He went back down the corridor with his parents. There wasn't much to tell.

'I have to get back to Emmy and Mia.'

'Yes,' his father said. 'We will come back tomorrow. Call us if you need anything, no matter what time.'

Micky nodded and watched his parents walk down the corridor. His mother rested her head on his father's shoulder as he kept her steady. He returned to his family.

Micky pulled the curtain back. Another chair, one more suitable for an overnight stay, was in the cubical along with a tray of sandwiches and two cups of coffee. He held Emmy's hand, all the improvement in her health had disappeared. She rested a hand on her belly as if she knew.

'Come on, eat something and then rest,' he said.

To his surprise, Emmy ate a sandwich and drank her coffee. He sat her on the lounge chair and said, 'You need to rest.'

She didn't say anything, just kept her eyes glued on Mia.

'I will watch over Mia,' he said.

Emmy closed her eyes. She was shivering, but she shouldn't be cold. He wrapped the blanket around her and held her hand until her grip loosened and her hand fell away from his. He tucked that hand under the blanket, sat on the other chair and watched over their daughter as he'd promised.

A butterfly brushing the back of his hand startled Micky. He lifted his head from his folded arms.

'Daddy,' Mia said.

He placed his hand on her forehead. She was still warm, but she wasn't burning up anymore.

'What?' Emmy jolted upright in the chair. He helped her from the lounge chair, sat her on one beside the bed and put Mia's little hand into hers.

The curtains pulled back, and medical staff entered the

cubicle. Dr Perez put his hand on Mia's forehead, checked her pulse while the machines recorded her vital signs. It had been a long night with the medical staff checking on Mia every half an hour, then every hour, Emmy waking each time.

'Well, you gave us quite a scare, young lady,' Dr Perez said.

Mia looked unsure at his comment. 'Mummy,' she said, 'did we miss the aeroplane?'

'Yes, we missed the plane, but it doesn't matter. There will be others,' Emmy said. She ran her hands through Mia's curls.

'Was Leo frightened on his own?'

'No, Leo is brave, like you. He wasn't frightened. He will be home with his daddy soon.'

Mia closed her eyes.

'No!' Emmy cried.

'It's okay. Let her rest,' the doctor told Emmy. 'She will be alright now. Her temperature has come down … the antibiotics are doing what they should.'

He placed his hand on Micky's shoulder. 'I have spoken to your commanding officer. You have time off to look after your family, and I'm told the Ambassador is sending a car for you.'

When they were alone, Micky folded his arms around Emmy's shoulders and covered her in his embrace. He would be forever grateful for the Adventist Hospital and the two wards set aside for US citizens after it was handed back to the South Vietnamese government in 1973.

Emmaline

'Go home, get cleaned up, have a rest and something to eat. I will stay with Mia,' Kate said later that day.

And they did, in the car the US Embassy sent for them, the car Kate had arrived in. They climbed the steps into Kate and Michael's empty apartment and collapsed into bed, covered in yesterday's grime.

Emmy woke before Micky, knowing he hadn't slept the night before. She pulled the sheet over him and went and showered. When she looked in the mirror, the dark circles under the eyes in the gaunt pale face staring back, startled her.

She tossed on a pair of old shorts and a t-shirt from her luggage before searching in the kitchen for coffee and food. Micky wrapped his arms around her as she did this, covered only by a towel around his waist. He no longer hid his scars from her. She placed her hand on the scar on his chest, and he lifted her hand to his lips and kissed her fingers.

'I love you,' he told her.

Emmy ran her hand across her face and into her lank hair.

'I love you,' Micky repeated.

Emmy curled into his body, and for that brief minute, the world disappeared. 'I love you,' she said.

She rested in Micky's embrace. 'I was so scared, Micky. What would have happened? What would I have done?'

He eased her back, looked into her eyes and said, 'Mia is okay. Remember that. She's okay. It's all going to be okay.' He placed his hand on her belly. 'You need to rest.'

'I know. Leo is safe. Mary-Anne will be alright.'

Micky said, 'I need you to rest, Emmy. You …need to …'

His eyes told her what she already knew, how much he loved her. They also told her what she hadn't understood until that moment. How much she held his life in her hands. What it was like for him to leave her, to stay away from her, to keep her safe. How easy it would be for him to slip back into the darkness; how he fought that darkness for her, never letting her see the fight.

Emmy curled back into his arms, turned her eyes away from the scars; she would not let Micky fight that darkness alone.

She looked up at him and said, 'I will rest.'

His body reacted to those words, and she felt him let go of the fear he was holding.

Emmy knew how to look after her family – she'd done that all her life – putting herself first was different.

Micky and her children, Mia and the unborn baby … must look after them.

Chapter Forty-one

Emmaline

Emmy read the telegram.

> *Leo arrived, safely. Thank you.*
>
> *Harry Johnson.*

On Saturday 19th April 1975: Emmy sat on a balcony overlooking Saigon, seeing what she hadn't seen before. The war was coming to an end: it was only a matter of when and how. Michael Brannigan had told her the North Vietnamese Army had agreed not to interfere in the evacuation of the US and other western citizens, as long as it was quick and without delays. She was one of those citizens.

Emmy and Mia were staying with Kate and Michael. It was safer at the apartment they rented, as an armed guard now stood at the building's entrance, Kate and Michael not the only Embassy staff living in that building.

Emmy knew Michael would not leave until the Ambassador did, and she knew Micky would be among the last to leave. She would be on her own until he joined her.

The anguish of the past days dogged her: how sick Mia had been; how afraid she had been; how Micky's love kept her together. She wanted more time but knew there wasn't more, and she didn't know how much time she had.

Mia rested in the bedroom where Kate was reading, but Emmy knew Kate making sure Mia was alright. Michael was at work at the Embassy and Micky was back on duty. A normal day, if she didn't look too closely. If she did, she would see the throngs of terrified people filling the city; she would hear the rumble of weapons firing in the background. She was grateful to Kate and Michael for the security they provided her and Mia, and for the comfort Micky had in knowing she was with them.

She folded the telegram, closed her eyes and slept.

On Sunday evening, Micky rushed in and out of her life. She heard him talking with his mother in the kitchen; she heard his footsteps as he checked Mia in the bedroom. He sat beside her on the couch in the living room, where she curled into his body. He pushed her hair away from her face, kissed her mouth and held her tight. He wasn't staying; they only had time to share coffee and a few words. Then he was gone.

On Monday, President Thieu of South Vietnam resigned, blaming the US for the fall of his government, for the fall of South Vietnam.

On Wednesday, the President of the United States, Gerald Ford, declared *the war is finished as far as America is concerned.*

On Thursday, Emmy had a visitor. She liked to sit on the balcony, but the war was too close, the air too thick, the traffic too loud, and the distress of the population too visible. Empty buildings were being ransacked, boards that protected windows were being pulled down and the glass smashed, awnings broken, cars abandoned.

Mary-Anne handed her a letter. 'It came in an embassy dispatch bag. The Ambassador said there won't be anymore.'

Emmy reached out. 'Thank you. What are you going to do?' Mary-Anne had been a source of strength and security for her — she was vulnerable now.

'The children?' Emmy asked.

'Holt International has offered help with our children. They have accommodation stateside where the children can live. I hope they will be cared for.'

'And you?'

'Three of our children have parents waiting in Australia. I will accompany them. The Australian Embassy is closing tomorrow, and the RAAF is flying out the remaining Australians.'

'I'm glad you have decided to leave. What will happen to the orphanage?'

'Sister Monica and Sister Rose will take over the orphanage. We have at least six months' supplies and enough money for wages, and the rent's paid. I hope there will be a peaceful settlement.'

Mary-Anne shook her head and said, 'How are you and Mia.'

Emmy took her hand. 'We are better. Mia is almost back to normal, and I can keep some food down.'

'When will you leave?'

'We are safe here at the moment. We will go when we are told.'

Emmy tried to keep the conversation light and bright; she couldn't let herself or anyone else know her fears.

After she farewelled Mary-Anne, she read the letter.

Dear Emmy,

My little boy has arrived safely. I cannot thank you enough. Leo tells me your daughter became ill and you missed the plane. I hope she is recovered.

My little boy has two brothers in Australia, and I wish one day he will meet them.

At the moment, he is distressed at all the changes in his life. He speaks of you and Mia, your little girl, I presume. His English, thanks to you and his mother, is reasonable.

He has seen a lot of changes in his short life; the farm

is beyond anything he could imagine. Our sheepdog had puppies, and I have given the littlest one to Leo as a pet. This has, I think, given him a sense of belonging. It is very early days.

I hope you will keep in touch. As I said, Leo speaks of Mia all the time.

Thank you again.

Harry

Emmy replied, unsure when she could post her letter.

Dear Harry,

Thank you for your letter.

Mia has recovered. It was a fright for her father and for me, but she seems to have suffered no lasting effects.

She is missing Leo as well; I hope we will be able to see him in the future. My parents live in Mosman Park near Perth so we will be not that far from you when we visit.

We expect to leave Vietnam any day; I am unsure as to our destination. My husband is a US Marine so we will evacuate as directed.

I hope the children we helped in Saigon will find peace and happiness. I am especially happy at finding you for Leo. I wish you both well.

I will help Mia write to Leo once we are home.

Yours sincerely,

Emmy

On Sunday 27th April 1975: rockets fell in downtown Saigon. Kate and Michael's apartment, though far enough away, registered the noise as a distant rumbling.

The Marines were sleeping in the sports centre at the embassy.

Micky was on duty, there being no more time for family. Michael worked late at night. The television had stopped broadcasting so Kate listened to the Armed Forces Radio for the evacuation signal.

Emmy tried to keep Mia distracted. The lies she told about thunder no longer rang true, even for a child.

On Monday: bombs dropped on Tan Son Nhut airport, and evacuation by plane ended. Kate and Emmy kept busy, filling their time. Michael obtained exit visas and documents for Emmy and Mia. She tucked them into her backpack.

Chapter Forty-two

Emmaline

On Tuesday: an urgent knock came on the door. The Marine guard who stood on duty at the building entrance stood there when Kate opened the door.

'Ma'am,' he said, 'you have to be ready to leave in ten minutes.'

'What?' Kate said. 'I haven't heard the signal.'

'Ma'am. A car is coming for you in ten minutes,' he stressed.

Emmy stood behind Kate at the door. She hadn't heard the signal either, something to do with the Bing Crosby song *White Christmas*. And Emmy had listened to the radio if Kate wasn't able to.

'Ma'am!' he repeated.

'Yes. Yes, we will be ready.'

Emmy shovelled Mia into the back seat of the car, trying to keep her eyes off the scene unfolding around her. Emmy had thrown a change of clothing for her, Kate and for Mia into the bottom of her backpack, making sure she had all her documents. Mia carried one doll. Kate carried her handbag, with her documents and a few essentials.

Saigon was not the city it had been when she'd arrived over six months ago. It had always been hectic and noisy, but it had been alive and green. Now it was dying, the streets covered in litter, broken glass and burnt-out cars. Discarded uniforms and weapons still lay around; no one seemed interested in picking them up. People roamed, some without purpose, while others were intent on taking what they wanted, breaking windows, stealing stock from stores. Some of the streets were quiet, others full of violence. Helicopters thumped in the dirty, dusty air.

Emmy held Mia close, the drive to the US Embassy taking too long, showing too much of the destruction years of conflict caused. Masses of people surged around the walls of the Embassy. The road to the gate was blocked, so the car could not move forward.

Vincent Garcia addressed Kate from the driver's seat, 'We will have to walk, Ma'am. Are you okay to walk?'

'Yes, I'm okay to walk,' Kate said.

'Mummy?' Mia queried, trembling, her eyes full of tears as they opened the car door into the crowd of people surrounding the Embassy.

'It's okay. I will carry you,' Emmy said.

'No, Mrs Brannigan,' Vincent said. 'I will carry her.'

He tossed Emmy's backpack over his shoulder and bent to pick Mia up.

'Mummy,' Mia cried.

'Daddy's friend will carry you,' Emmy told her daughter.

Mia let Vincent pick her up and carry her towards the embassy gate, Kate following close behind. The crowd pushed and shoved into them. Vincent put his arm around Kate; checked that Emmy was one step behind him.

Then he was gone. Emmy was alone, standing, staring, a woman in front of her urging her to take her baby, pushing the child into Emmy's arms.

'I can't,' Emmy said. 'I'm sorry, I can't.' She craned her neck, trying to see through the crowd ahead of her. Emmy saw that Vincent had reached the gate; saw him jostle Mia and Kate through the opening.

She tried to move; tried to move the woman away, to get to her child. She did understand; she also knew there was nothing she could do. The crowd surrounded her, suffocating her. 'I can't,' she repeated.

The woman and baby disappeared, pushed away by the crowd as it stampeded around her. Emmy lost her footing, and the swell carried her away, away from Mia, away from safety. She tripped, but something grabbed her arms, stopping her fall.

'I'm here,' Micky said.

Micky

Micky was hot and covered in sweat and dirt. He'd shoved the crowd away with a fierceness he didn't know he was capable of, a fierceness he struggled to control. But he had to get to Emmy. And now he stood watching them as he held her in his arms. He wasn't armed; he'd left his pistol behind the wall for safety, to ensure no one could take it from him.

The crowd of civilians desperate for help to leave had too many men of military age in it. An angry crowd, frantic and afraid, feeling abandoned, but not unwise. They wanted entry to the gate; they wanted the safety that gate would give them, the escape that gate would give them. Hurting him would not get them that.

He should be safe. Emmy should be safe.

'I'm here,' he said again, holding her close and steadying her.

She leant on him, using his body as support and, when he lifted her into his arms, she clung to him like she was Mia, her arms around his neck, her legs wrapped around his back.

'Micky,' she whispered.

The crowd made way for him as he carried her towards the gate, but as he got closer, they became agitated. The gate must open to let him in. If they pushed hard enough, there could be a chance of entry, of safety.

'I'm okay. I can walk,' she told him, so he lowered her to the ground. She swayed unsteadily on her feet, so he put his arm around her waist and held her upright, protecting her from the surrounding mass.

The gate opened just enough for him to bundle her through, then he pulled it shut again. The crowd pushed and shoved the metal structure, trying to keep it open, but the Marines on the other side held it firm.

Micky turned to face the crowd. Here, he should be safe.

'Brannigan!' He heard his name called. He looked up at the wall; saw his buddy leaning over the parapet, rifle in hand. He scrambled along the edge of the entrance, took the arm offered and hurled himself up onto the wall.

'Mummy!' he heard Mia call and saw Emmy kneeling, her hand resting on the ground. He saw his parents rushing to her aid.

Jumping down from the wall into the embassy grounds, he ran to his family.

'Daddy!' Mia cried and ran to him. He scooped her up. And she sobbed in his arms.

'Hush, hush,' he tried to soothe her.

His father helped Emmy up and held her steady. She was pale, her body shaking, but she didn't look hurt.

'It's okay, Mia. I've got you,' he told his daughter.

Emmaline

How quiet everything seemed inside the walls. The chaos outside the gate, the noise, the terror, desperate people looking for a way inside seemed to disappear. Behind the wall, away from the gate, those who had made it to safety – and there were many hundreds, possibly thousands – sat quietly, almost numb. Occasionally, a child cried.

Then the whack, whack, whack of helicopter blades shattered the air and the quiet as people scrambled aboard, and their screeching engines took off again.

Micky carried Mia towards Emmy, and she saw him talking to

her; saw Mia stop shuddering in her father's arms.

In the shadow of the Embassy's fourteen-foot wall, Emmy rested against Michael Brannigan's shoulder as her husband stood in front of his father. Emmy saw the look that passed between them, the old warrior and the young warrior. She heard his mother stifle a cry. Kate understood that look. Emmy took her own weight as Micky said to Mia, 'I want you to go with Grandpa. You have to go with Grandpa.'

'Daddy!'

Micky put Mia into his father's arms.

'Hush now. You're okay,' Michael Brannigan said as he took his granddaughter from his son.

Micky embraced his father, held his mother tight and watched as they moved away with his daughter.

Then they were alone.

Micky's hands checked Emmy for injuries. His face, covered in dirt and dust, looked like he hadn't slept for days. He was unkempt and unshaven, and his uniform was filthy, not how he wanted to present himself; Emmy knew that.

'I'm okay. I'm not hurt,' she said.

'Stay with my parents, Emmy,' he said.

'Yes … I'm … I will.'

A landing helicopter stirred up more dirt, further destroying the quiet as they stood together, their eyes locked.

Emmy leant into Micky's chest. When it was quiet enough to talk, he eased her away and said, 'I'm sorry, I will be with you as soon as I can. Stay with my parents,' he repeated.

She nodded.

'I love you,' Micky said. 'I will always be with you, no matter what.'

'And I will always be with you.' Emmy said

Micky kissed her lips, then touched his lips to her forehead. Then Kate was there, her hand on Emmy's arm. 'Come on now,' she said.

Micky pulled out of her arms.

Dirt and dust flew in Emmy's eyes, and noise assaulted her ears as another helicopter landed. She watched the back of her husband as he walked away. Emmy wrapped her arms around her stomach, holding herself together.

We will not be alone, she told her unborn child.

Chapter Forty-three

Emmaline

Emmy watched Kate and Michael say goodbye. After thirty years together, she was leaving him behind; leaving her son behind. Emmy helped Kate into the helicopter where they sat together, alone in a crowd of frightened refugees. Mia closed her eyes and slept the sleep of fear and exhaustion.

The helicopter ride out over the South China Sea could have been beautiful. The sun was setting over the land and sea, glistening on the blue water and sending trails of gold and silver along the waves. But the sky was also full of aircraft and noise.

On the deck of the command ship, helicopters that had run out of fuel were being pushed overboard, making room for the incoming flights. The night sky was full of lights, noise and helicopters. Lines of people covered the ship's deck, using a guiding rope as they were led below.

After they landed, an officer with greying blond hair met them. Kate fell into his arms as she stepped off the aircraft.

'Joe,' she said.

He escorted them off the deck away from the crowds, a young sailor carrying Mia behind them. Mia clung to her doll, no longer objecting to the strangeness of the situation she was in. Emmy walked beside them, stroking Mia's hair.

The cabin they were shown into was cool and quiet, an officer's cabin by the photos and mementos around the room.

Admiral Joseph Daniels hugged Emmy like she was someone he'd been waiting a long time to meet.

'There is coffee. I will arrange some food for you,' he said. 'I have to go … I can't stay, I'm sorry.'

'Joe….' Kate queried.

'Not yet,' he replied.

Kate appeared to shrink at this, but she pulled herself up straight and said, 'Thank you.'

'I'll let you know,' he said.

He held Kate tight again before he left the cabin.

Emmy was too tired to eat, but Kate insisted. The coffee was good, reminding her of the first time she'd had coffee with Micky. It seemed a lifetime ago.

Mia ate and Emmy washed her face and hands and put her on the bed in the cabin, where she slept. Emmy lay down beside her and, to her surprise, she slept too.

The knock on the door woke her.

Kate had slept on the couch in the corner of the room. She was startled, woken by the noise. Standing, she straightened her skirt before answering the door.

'Ma'am, the Admiral said to let you know the Ambassador is on his way. He should be landing in about ten minutes.'

'Thank you.'

Kate closed the door, and Emmy saw her lean against it and put her hand to her face before she turned to check on her and Mia. Emmy swung her legs over the side of the bed and stood. She wrapped Kate in her arms.

'Go and wait for him,' she said. 'We are okay.'

'I don't … Micky …' Kate said.

'Micky will leave last,' Emmy said.

Kate nodded. Glancing at the mirror hanging on the wall, she ran her hands through her untidy hair; touched her dirty, pale cheeks.

'Go and wait for him,' Emmy repeated.

When she was alone, she wiped her tears away and sat on the couch, grateful Mia still slept.

And there she waited.

Chapter Forty-four

Micky

Micky had spent Tuesday morning pulling up trees to make landing areas for helicopters. He wasn't sure if he'd slept last night or the night before, the days and nights now rolling into each other. He'd spent time driving buses around, picking up designated evacuees. He'd spent time guarding the incinerator on the roof where millions of dollars and documents were being burnt. And he'd heard two of his comrades had died when a bomb had dropped on their guard post at the airport.

Later in the afternoon, he'd been on the embassy wall helping authorised evacuees – Vietnamese who'd helped the US, and those the US had helped, US citizen and their families, and citizens of allied countries – over the wall into the compound. Women and children were helped through the gate.

If he hadn't been on the wall, he wouldn't have seen Emmy. He'd pushed and shoved to get to her; he had carried her back to the gate; he couldn't let her climb over the fence. He'd left her in the care of his parents and returned to his duty.

Thousands of people were gathered outside the Embassy; more than two thousand were in the compound. Reinforcements had arrived by helicopter to help the Embassy Marines with their duties. Helicopters were constantly evacuating those inside the compound.

At 19.00 hours, his commanding officer called him to his office. 'Your wife and child have evacuated,' he told Micky. 'Your mother is with them.'

His commanding officer reached out and took his arm. 'They are safe now,' he said.

Emmy and Mia were safe. He could concentrate now on what he had to do.

Clouds covered the sky as the last of the daylight faded. The car park and embassy grounds were well lit by vehicles with their lights on. He'd taken time to eat. There was no time to sleep.

Micky helped a woman and her children onto a helicopter, the oldest boy sobbing. The younger one was quiet, stunned into silence; he clutched Micky's hand as they crouched under the still blades of a helicopter. The baby in the woman's arms, thankfully, was too young to know what was going on. He helped the woman into the aircraft, put her baby on her knee and sat her children beside her. There was nothing else for him to do. They were too frightened, too distraught to know he was there.

He thought of Mia safe on a ship off the coast. She would have a home, a family. How many of these children were leaving their fathers, their families, behind.

Helicopters were leaving the embassy every ten minutes.

At three in the morning, the crowd around the embassy grew larger and more agitated, knowing the evacuation was taking place, knowing there was not enough time for all those wanting to evacuate. The evacuation would end soon, the North Vietnamese army close to a victory.

Micky saw from his position on the wall, South Vietnamese soldiers strip their uniforms off and toss them away. Some raced away in underwear, even discarding their boots. He understood: they needed to protect themselves, protect their families.

No one knew what would happen, but he knew. He'd seen the brutality of war, his body and mind scared forever by it. All the deaths and injuries, physical and mental. Simon's death always in his mind.

The North Vietnamese Army would soon control Saigon.

There could only be a few hours before that happened.

At four-thirty, Micky was part of a semicircle around the parking lot. Then he was moved into the embassy building to prepare for evacuation. That's when the crowd outside broke through the Embassy gates.

Micky raced up the stairwell with his detachment, stopping at each floor to bolt the gates and doors on the way up to the roof. From the sixth-floor roof, he saw a water tanker crash through the embassy's ground floor. Saw looters carry away furniture of all shapes and sizes. He heard gunshots in the air.

At 4.58, the US Ambassador, Graham Martin, evacuated. Micky knew his father would be on that flight.

The door to the stairwell on the rooftop was sealed.

At 6.45, the sun was coming up, and the heat came with it. Micky waited on the rooftop with his detachment. By now, helicopters had stopped coming to the embassy.

Micky could see the streets of Saigon. He could see cars burning, discarded uniforms, weapons and boots. He could hear angry shouting in the stairwell. The door would not stay secure for much longer.

Marines would do their duty. They would protect themselves and each other. A bottle of whisky was being passed around. Micky sat quietly. He wrote on a scrap of notepad:

> *My darling,*
>
> *Forgive me for letting you down. I will love you forever, no matter where I am, no matter what happens to me. I will miss you and my little girl. Help her understand I love her and how I wish I could have seen her grow up. Our baby, yet to be born, I should be there with you like I promised. I'm sorry I cannot go back to that prison I hope you can you forgive me for being such a coward. You will always have my heart, my soul, my love. I will always be with you.*

I love you.

Micky

Micky folded the paper and put it in his top pocket. He hoped his body would be found and that Emmy would get his letter. It was only a hope.

He took the whisky bottle from Vincent Garcia, his hand steady, but the young Marine's trembled. Micky grasped his arm and held it tight; looked into his eyes. He knew his decision was his to make. Vincent would make his own decision. Dying wasn't the worst thing that could happen.

Micky could die on this rooftop, or he could go back to prison, to beatings, torture, and darkness. Emmy loved him; she would forgive him if he did not survive.

The door on the stairwell began to bulge.

Too late for rescue, they would fight for their lives or be handed over as prisoners.

Micky picked up his weapon. *I'm sorry, Emmy, forgive me. Look after our children. I love you.*

Emmaline

Micky, no, please ….

Emmy stumbled and leant on the railing on the command ship. The sun was coming up. The ship's engines were starting up, the deck busy with sailors. She had found a corner out of the way. The noise of helicopters had faded away since the Ambassador had come aboard.

Michael and Kate had come back to the cabin.

Emmy's stomach heaved, and Kate had said, 'Go up and get some air. We will mind Mia.'

'Emmaline,' Michael Brannigan called as he crossed the deck. He walked with a purpose, not showing what he must have been feeling.

'Are you alright?'

Emmy turned to face him.

'Micky can't go back to that prison, can he?' she asked.

'He can't,' Michael said.

She whimpered, and Michael Brannigan put his arm around her. 'No one will be left behind,' he said.

But the ship was moving away from the coast. The sun was beating down; the air hot.

He repeated, 'No one will be left behind.' Was it for her or for him, she wondered? She leant into his shoulder, held his arm tight around her. She could not cry; she had no tears left.

'Mummy,' Mia called as she came across the deck of the ship, holding her grandmother's hand.

Emmy bent and cuddled her child.

'Where's Daddy?' Mia asked.

Emmy looked at the coast that was getting further away. Sweat moistened her brow as she steadied her hands and said, 'He is coming, Mia.'

'Where?' Mia asked.

Emmy stood and locked eyes with Michael Brannigan, his arms around Kate as she stared at the vanishing land.

Emmy crouched down to face Mia and said, 'Daddy will be on another ship. No one gets left behind.'

Chapter Forty-five

Emmaline

A week later, Michael Brannigan carried his granddaughter onto a flight out of Manila. No-one stopped him. No one asked him for her papers. Emmy's US passport and Michael's diplomatic status ensured they travelled to safety.

Emmy could have gone to San Francisco with Kate and Michael, but she went home to Australia, to her parents, to her brothers. To the green trees that never lost their leaves and the blue sky that went on forever, to the eucalyptus in the air, and the land she missed under her feet.

On a cold winter's day in the middle of June, Emmy folded a letter and put it in the pocket of her black duffle coat. She wiped her tears and stared out at the ocean. Between her and the sea, Mia built sandcastles. There was no one else on the beach.

Lightning from a storm sitting on the horizon flashed in the sky. The wind would start blowing if the storm moved closer to land. They would then have to leave.

Mia should be at school, but she had only started sleeping during the night. Emmy would not hurry her – school could wait. Emmy would wait.

Wind blew across the water, and Emmy began gathering their bits and pieces together.

Emmaline. The wind blew her name around.

Mia looked up from her sandcastle, up across the sand that

hadn't washed away in previous storms; she looked past the walkway they were sitting under to the lawn.

Emmaline.

'Daddy!' Mia cried. She jumped up from her sandcastle and ran.

Emmy fumbled with her bag; dropped the contents onto the sand. She stood still, staring; she couldn't move. If she moved, the scene might disappear if she was dreaming.

The second night on the command ship, the admiral had come to the cabin. Kate had cried, and Michael had crossed the room. Mia had looked up from her drawing, while Emmy had gripped the arms of the chair she sat in.

She could not … would not … ask Micky to go back to that prison, to the beatings, to the torture. She would live without Micky before she asked him to do that.

Michael knelt in front of her.

'Micky's safe,' he'd said.

'Safe,' Emmy repeated.

Michael had nodded.

Micky's letters arrived every other day, sometimes a brief note, other times pages. *I'm sorry it's taking so long,* he had written in his last letter.

Now he ran across the sand. Dropping his kit bag, he picked up Mia, swung her around and carried her back to Emmy.

He stood in front of Emmy. Mia whispered in his ear, and he put her on the sand and took Emmy's face in his hands; put his lips to hers.

She wasn't dreaming.

Micky

The bird in the sky, the one Micky had seen from the Embassy rooftop, was a rescue helicopter, one of the last to leave Saigon.

He'd been able to get a message to his father so Emmy knew he was alive; she'd not had to read his letter – he'd torn it to pieces and thrown it in the ocean.

After he'd slept, he'd put his weapons down, sought out his commanding officer and offered his help.

It had taken a week to reach Manila, where he'd applied for leave and spent the next six weeks in Guam helping with refugees.

When his leave came through, he jagged a flight earlier than expected. He had no Australian coin on the stopover in Sydney, so Emmy didn't know he was on his way.

Micky held her face, lowered his head and put his lips on hers. Her lips were cold, but dark circles no longer sat under her eyes. Their kiss was the most precious he'd ever shared.

'I knew you would be here,' he said. He hadn't gone to the house in Fremantle but had come straight to Cottesloe Beach from the airport.

'Yes,' Emmy said.

He pulled her into his embrace, their unborn child obviously growing. He put his hand on her belly. Then Mia reached for his hand, and he picked her up and wrapped them both in his arms.

Emmy trembled, and he turned his back to the storm coming in over the ocean, sheltering his family.

He was alive, his family in his arms. 'I'm here,' he said. He would be with Emmy. He would keep his promise to Emmy.

'You will not be alone,' he said. 'I'm home.'

And he was.

Micky was home.

Epilogue

Emmy stood beside Micky. The reflection in the black granite showed a girl with flowers in her hair, wearing a calico blouse and long floral skirt. Showed a young man dressed in a white naval uniform.

Micky reached out and placed his hand on the name: Simon Daniels. One of more than 58,000 names on the wall. Emmy covered his hand with hers.

'It was never about the soldiers,' Emmy said.

'I know,' he replied. He dropped to his knees, and Emmy knelt beside him; rested her forehead on his.

*****

Jasmine Simone Brannigan held her sister's hand as their parents remembered. At ten years old, she looked nothing like her father or older sister, Mia. She looked like her mother with fair hair and hazel eyes.

Her seven-year-old twin brothers sat at the foot of the granite monument and pushed miniature flags into the ground. One held the stars and stripes, the other, the Australian flag.

They had dark hair and brown eyes, like their father, Michael Francis Brannigan, Registered Nurse, Repatriation General Hospital, Nedlands, Western Australia.

The End

About the Author

Western Australian-born Bernadette lives in Secret Harbour, Western Australia, with her husband and a very old cranky ginger cat her daughter rescued. She backpacked around Europe in the mid-seventies and still likes to travel and visit her youngest, who lives in Berlin. When she is not being a mum of three, grand-mum of three, wife, or daughter, she spends her time writing.

Tomorrow's Promise came out of her experiences living in Perth in the late sixties and early seventies. They were chaotic times. When some were looking for a better way. When your life and those around you could be changed by the drop of a lottery ball and you could be sent off to war. When a protest against war was not a protest against those who fought and died.